Amy Cross is the author of more than 200 horror, paranormal, fantasy and thriller novels.

OTHER TITLES
BY AMY CROSS INCLUDE

1689
American Coven
Annie's Room
The Ash House
Asylum
B&B
The Bride of Ashbyrn House
The Cemetery Ghost
The Curse of the Langfords
The Devil, the Witch and the Whore
Devil's Briar
The Disappearance of Lonnie James
Eli's Town
The Farm
The Ghost of Molly Holt
The Ghosts of Lakeforth Hotel
The Girl Who Never Came Back
Haunted
The Haunting of Blackwych Grange
The Haunting of Nelson Street
The House on Fisher Street
The House Where She Died
Out There
Stephen
The Shades
The Soul Auction
Trill

THE SIXTH WINDOW

THE CHRONICLES OF SISTER JUNE BOOK SIX

AMY CROSS

CONTENTS

THE
SIXTH
WINDOW

PROLOGUE

1982...

"IT'S BEAUTIFUL," SISTER JOSEPHINE said, as she sat in her wheelchair on the viewing platform above the main workshop. "Or at least, it *will* be beautiful. When it's finished."

Before her, a dozen technicians were examining the fragments that had been removed from the cavern under the Sahara. Some of those fragments were little more than small pieces of dust, while others were larger and had been assembled at the far end of the workshop. Slowly but surely, the gate from beneath the desert was being reassembled.

"We've got teams beavering away around

the clock," Cardinal Abruzzo explained. "They work in three shifts, so there's always someone here, day and night. I happen to think that they've made remarkable progress so far. It's like the world's hardest but most important jigsaw puzzle."

"It's starting to look like a gate," Josephine whispered, her eyes filled with a growing sense of anticipation. "How much longer do you think we need to wait?"

"This work can't be rushed," he told her.

"But how long?"

"I think we can have the larger parts in place by the end of the year, and then -"

"I need it sooner!" she snapped angrily. "Do I look like someone who can afford to think in terms of years? I want the gate reassembled within the week."

"That is simply impossible," he told her.

"For you, perhaps, and your paltry team, but I shall simply have to find better workers." She tried to lift herself from the wheelchair, only to struggle for a few seconds before slumping back down. "This wretched body isn't going to last for much longer. All these years later, I'm still suffering from the injuries I received in the snow." She paused for a moment, her eyes filling with tears as she watched a technician carrying a tiny fragment of stone over to the gate. "I've worked too hard to fail now," she purred. "Can you imagine what it would be like to work for one clear goal, and to fail before you reach your moment of triumph?"

"I can't," Cardinal Abruzzo replied, "but... I must still warn you that we need to be patient. The team have already gone down several dead ends that cost them hours of work, and going any faster would risk causing damage to the structure." He paused, before placing a hand on her shoulder. "I know how hard this is for you, Sister Josephine. I know it's difficult. But please, I'm begging you, let us do our work at the correct pace. The end result will be so much greater than if we rush."

"I must be the first to pass through that gate when it's finished," she told him, still staring down at the workshop with a faraway gaze. "Others will come after me, but I must be first."

"And you shall be," he said firmly. "By the way, the other matter we discussed recently is also proceeding as planned. In fact, I don't think it could possibly be going any better."

Josephine continued to watch the progress of the technicians as two of them knelt at one side of the gate. After a few more seconds, however, she emerged from her daze and looked up to see a faint smile on Cardinal Abruzzo's face.

"Are you talking about that idiotic woman?" she snarled.

He nodded.

"She allowed the gate to become damaged in the first place," she continued, her voice dripping now with contempt. "She didn't know its significance, but still, she should have had better sense. Now that we no longer require her for our work, I hope that she's being suitably punished."

"I still think we should have just had her killed," he replied. "A bullet to the back of the head would have been easy enough to arrange. Or, if you were worried, we could have arranged various accidents while she was returning to this country. After all, that's how we've been planning to get rid of all the other operatives."

"But I want her to suffer for what she did to me!" she hissed. "I want her to pay! And after reading her file, I realized immediately how we can drive her out of her mind! Death would be too good for Sister June." She held up her right hand, wincing with pain as she struggled to clench a fist. "I want her to taste the agony that she caused me when she rebelled in Switzerland all those years ago. Not just physical pain, either, but something deeper and darker. I want to shatter her mind!"

"That process is very much underway as we

speak," he replied, making a point of checking his watch. "The delays of the past few weeks were unwanted, but ultimately they will pay off perfectly. We even had time to add a few finishing flourishes, such as putting up an old photograph that some fool bodged together many years ago. There are a lot of moving pieces that had to be put in place at Holdham Hall, plus Shadborne wasn't quite ready just yet."

"Is it now?"

"It is."

"And where is Sister June?"

"As we speak, I believe she is in a car, being driven to Holdham Hall. Once she's there, I can't see any way that she could ever possibly escape. I've been over the paperwork many times, and I'm absolutely confident that I've worked out exactly how to make her suffer. Give it a few days, and I should be able to deliver some very good news."

"I want proof," Josephine told him wearily, as he took hold of her wheelchair and steered her away from the viewing platform. "I want a live feed showing me what happens to her when she reaches Shadborne. I want to watch as her mind breaks, and I want to hear her cries of pain. And then, once I finally decide that the time has come to let her die, I want to pass through that gate and lead the greatest army the world has ever seen!"

CHAPTER ONE

THICK MIST HUNG IN the night air, covering the lawn and almost entirely obscuring the house beyond. Occasional gaps in the mist, however, revealed a few details of the building: a turret here, a window there, and on the southern side a low extension with several doors set into its side. This was a scene that had remained undisturbed for many years.

Slowly two beams of light began to cut through the darkness, accompanied a few seconds later by the sound of a car's wheels grinding along the driveway. The headlights caught the front of the house, with its imposing black door, as the vehicle came to a halt with the engine still running. Had anyone been looking at one of the windows at the exact right moment, they might have spotted just the faintest hint of a figure moving in the darkness beyond.

***

"Well, this is it," Parks said, still making no move to switch the engine off as he peered out at the house ahead. He checked the map again. "Yes, this is definitely it. It doesn't look too inviting, though, does it? Perhaps there's been a mistake and -"

"There has been no mistake," June replied, interrupting him before she had a chance to stop herself. "This is indeed Holdham Hall."

"My instructions were to drop you here and leave immediately," Parks muttered, squinting as he looked at the front door, "but I'm not sure that quite sits with me. It must be very cold in there, and you're..."

He turned to her, and for a moment he looked her up and down rather conspicuously.

"Well," he continued, "no offense, but you're just..."

"A woman?" she replied, raising an eyebrow.

"Well, that too," he said, "but I was meaning more... you're just..."

"A nun?"

"It's hard to miss."

"I can assure you that I'm more than capable of taking care of myself," she told him. "Why, only recently I was out in the Sahara."

"You were, huh?" He seemed genuinely impressed by that news. "I bet it was a damn sight warmer there."

She turned to him.

"Pardon my language," he added. "Listen, I'm really not sure I can just drop you off here and drive away, it doesn't seem right." He reached for the key in the ignition. "Let me at least come inside with you and check that there aren't any -"

"No!" she said, reaching over and taking his hand, making sure that he couldn't touch the key. "Absolutely not Your instructions were quite clear on that point, were they not?"

"They were, but -"

"And what are you suppose to do?"

"I'm supposed to drop you off and immediately leave, but -"

"Then I really don't see why there has to be any confusion," she said, opening the door on her side of the vehicle and stepping out, then opening the door behind and reaching in to pull out her suitcase. "Thank you very much for driving me here, Mr. Parks, I do hope it wasn't too far out of your way." As she took hold of the suitcase's handle, she fumbled slightly as her hands began to tremble. "I trust that you will have a safe and pleasant ride home, and I can only apologize for the fact that you've been kept up so late."

"It's only eleven," he said, glancing at his watch. "I'm not sure that -"

"Excellent," she replied, pulling the suitcase out and swinging the door shut. She took a deep breath, and then she stepped toward the front of the car. "I'm afraid I'm not carrying any money, so I can't offer you a gratuity, but you have my unending gratitude. Thank you again."

Parks opened his mouth to reply, but June was already making her way across the grass, heading toward the house's front door.

"Weird," he said finally. "This is one weird situation, that's for sure." He watched as June stopped on the other side of the grass, seemingly transfixed by the sight of the front door, and for a few seconds he wondered whether she was actually going to go inside or not. "I've done a lot of chauffeur jobs in my day," he continued under his breath, "but driving some nun out to a seemingly abandoned house in the middle of the night... I think this particular job might just take the biscuit."

A moment later June turned and looked back at him, and in that instant Parks realized that this was his cue to leave. He waved at her, and she waved back, and then he put the car into reverse.

***

Standing on the gravel driveway, trying not to shiver lest she might be seem scared, June watched as the car's taillights disappeared into the distance. Once they were gone she waited a few more seconds, just in case they might return, before turning to look up at the house again.

"Well," she whispered, trying to hide the fear in her voice, "here we are once more. This is a most unusual turn of events, is it not? I can't help feeling that..."

Her voice trailed off for a moment as she felt her suspicions return. Had the First Order truly sent her to the house on some innocent mission, or had they known all along that this was the very same building in which she had spent her formative years? She felt sure that the First Order must have done plenty of research, that they probably knew her life story better than she knew it herself, and she supposed that this was too much of a coincidence to truly believe that it had come about by chance.

Indeed, she couldn't help wondering whether it might in fact be some kind of test. But would the First Order be so cruel?

"I just have to tell you," the young man at the airport had explained, "that there's been a change of plans. The person on the phone said you'd understand. A car will be waiting for you at Heathrow, and apparently it won't be taking you directly back to the convent. Does that make sense?"

After that there had been a brief diversion, and June had felt as if she'd been placed in a holding pattern before finally she'd been delivered to the house. And while the coincidences seemed to be stacking up, she couldn't help but think back to the mysterious voice she'd heard deep beneath the Sahara, a voice that had somehow known about one of her darkest secrets.

"This is where you've always belonged," the voice had told her. "You know that, deep down, if you search your soul. You know it's true... Since Holdham Hall. Since you were young. You've always known that you belong down here with us."

And she'd seen the place, too. Somehow, down in those tunnels, she'd briefly found herself back inside the very same house that she saw now. Although she wasn't entirely sure that such things were possible, she felt as if everything in recent weeks and months had been slowly converging to this point, as if some combination of destiny and the First Order had been determined to deliver her to this moment, as if they were keen for her to face a moment of reckoning for something that had happened many years earlier.

"I suppose I always knew this moment would come," she said now, through gritted teeth. "One cannot always outrun one's -"

Suddenly the front door burst open, and June was shocked to see another nun stepping out from the house's darkened interior.

"Oh, there you are!" the other woman stammered, clearly a little befuddled as she reached up to straighten her glasses. "I thought I heard a car! I'm -"

Before she could finish, she somehow dislodged the glasses from her face, sending them to the floor, where they tumbled down the steps and landed with both lenses shattered at June's feet.

"Oh," the other woman continued, "dear, that's really not... I wasn't trying to do that. No, not at all. Bother, that's going to be really rather a problem, I'm afraid. I'm blind as a bat without my glasses, and I'm afraid I don't have a spare pair with me." She patted her own pockets for a moment.

"Nope," she added, "my spare pair must be on my desk, but that's all the way back at my home, which is simply at the other end of the country. I'm so foolish, I usually bring at least one spare set, but everything was such a rush on this occasion and -"

Stopping suddenly, she squinted as she peered at June.

"Are you Sister June?" she asked, before picking her way very carefully down the steps and then reaching out a hand. "I was told to expect you. I hope your journey went well. My name is Sister Lucy. Welcome to Holdham Hall!"

CHAPTER TWO

1945...

"WELCOME," MRS. BARKER SAID, staring down at June from the top step outside the school, "to Holdham Hall, young lady. I trust that you are going to behave?"

Looking back up at the woman, June – just ten years old – had no idea what she was supposed to say in return. In general she'd always been told to keep quiet, yet she felt as if some kind of response was required. A moment later, hearing an engine disappearing into the distance, she turned just in time to see the motor car bumping away along the drive and disappearing around the corner.

"Well?" Mrs. Barker continued.

June turned to her, worried that she'd already made a terrible mistake.

"You're going to have to wipe that gormless look off your face," Mrs. Barker said, rolling her eyes before turning and stepping back through the open doorway. "I can't stand children who are unable to hide their naivety. I'm afraid you and I are in grave danger of getting off to a very bad start. Chop chop! Come along!"

"Yes!" June blurted out, hurrying up the stairs.

"And don't forget your case!"

"No!"

June turned, almost slipping, and hurried down. She grabbed her suitcase, before carrying it back up the stairs and disappearing through the door that led into Holdham Hall.

***

"You'll find discipline here, young lady," Mrs. Barker said as she stormed along the corridor, with June struggling to keep up behind her. "We take wayward and stray young girls and we change them so that they're ready to go out into the world. In your particular case, I think there's only one way to start."

"What's that?" June asked breathlessly, just about managing to lug her suitcase past the various closed doors on either side.

"I can tell that you're going to be trouble," Mrs. Barker told her.

"I don't want to be trouble."

"What you want is neither here nor there."

"I'm very grateful to you for letting me come here," June continued. "I was told that no-one wanted me."

"Don't assume that anyone wants you yet," Mrs. Barker continued, quickening her pace a little as her heels tapped loudly against the chipped tile floor. "One has to earn that distinction. Do you understand, June? One isn't born into this world with any rights or with anything owed to one. These are all things for which you must work, and that will be particularly difficult if you're not accustomed to such things.

"Of course, and -"

"And let me be quite clear about one other thing," Mrs. Barker said, stopping suddenly and turning to June, who almost crashed straight into her. "You are an orphan, are you not?"

"I... I am," June said, staring up at her.

"Well, I don't care," Mrs. Barker explained. "I'm not interested. Your parents died in the war but that doesn't matter at all." She let out a heavy, laborious sigh that was clearly intended to make some kind of point. "There are some people in this world who are of the opinion that orphans require special treatment. That they should be pitied or coddled in some way. I believe that those people are fools of the highest order. You will receive no special treatment from me, young lady, and you should not expect any from others."

"Okay," June stammered.

"Your father died in France and your mother was killed in an air-raid," Mrs. Barker continued, "but any sob stories were left at the door when you entered this school. From now on you're expected to stand on your own two feet, and if you even attempt once to curry favor by referring to your troubled past, you shall receive six lashes. Is that understood?"

"Yes," June said, flinching slightly at the mere thought of such horrible punishment.

"You're a weak and feeble little thing, aren't you?" Mrs. Barker mused, stepping around June and looking her up and down. "You don't seem built for hard manual labor, but at the same time you don't seem to have much of a brain."

"No," June said, feeling distinctly uneasy. "I mean... I'm sorry."

"It's hard to know what to make of you at all, or what to use you for. You seem utterly unhelpful in every regard. Tell me, do you have any skills that I should know about?"

"I don't think so," June admitted.

"As I thought," Mrs. Barker continued, stopping in front of her again, "you're utterly unremarkable. You don't have a special or interesting bone in your body, do you?"

"I... don't think so. Not that I'm aware of, any way."

"We'll find *something* for you to do, though," the older woman continued. "There's a saying of which I'm rather fond. Not everybody can be a wall, some have to make do with being mere bricks. And some, the lowest of the low, must be content to be nothing more than dust. You, June, are clearly dust."

"I am?" June replied, still struggling terribly to keep up with everything she was hearing. "Oh. I didn't know that."

"You didn't?"

June shook her head.

"Lord, give me strength," Mrs. Barker murmured. "This child is clearly several sandwiches short of a picnic."

"What does that mean?" June asked. "Is -"

"Silence!" Mrs. Barker shouted, slapping the side of her face with such force that June pulled back and tripped, landing with a thud on the floor. "Don't question me all the time," she continued, "it's very tiring. If you don't know the answer to a question, or if you don't understand what one of your superiors is saying, simply keep your mouth shut and don't make some rotten display of your ignorance. Is that clear?"

"Yes," June sobbed, unable to hold back tears as she touched her cheek. "I'm sorry."

"And don't be sorry all the time, either," the woman grumbled. "That's tiring as well! I can tell that you've got a lot to learn, young lady, but you'll learn it here. You're going to be sleeping in room thirty on the top floor, which you should be able to find easily enough, even with your limited intelligence. You'll attend classes during the day, but in the early mornings and evenings you'll be expected to work for your board and lodgings." She took a step forward, almost bumping June with the toes of her shoes in the process. "Is that understood?"

"Yes," June replied, struggling to keep from crying as she felt the slap still stinging her cheek. "I promise, Mrs Barker, I won't cause trouble. That's the last thing I'd ever want to do, I only want to fit in and help."

"We'll see about that," the woman said, turning her eyes and walking away. "Room thirty!" she called back to June. "You really shouldn't have any trouble finding it, but if you do, ask somebody else for directions. I don't want you coming to me with endless questions. In fact, I don't want to see you at all until this evening, when I shall give you some work to do. Is that clear?"

"Yes," June stammered, still shocked by the slap she'd received.

"Now get up off the floor," Mrs. Barker said, turning and storming away. "It's filthy down there. Don't you have any idea of how you're supposed to behave?"

"I'm sorry," June continued, hauling herself up. "I won't do it again."

As she watched Mrs. Barker disappearing around the corner, June couldn't help but feel that her arrival at the school couldn't have gone worse. She knew she had been a terrible disappointment, and she told herself that she simply had to try to do better; she supposed that Mrs. Barker was always right, and that therefore she had been entirely correct to strike June in such a harsh manner. Still feeling the sting on her face, June knew that she had to hold back her tears, so as she picked up the suitcase she resolved to never again show any sign of weakness or failure.

Instead, she turned and set off to try to find room thirty, and she told herself that she had to locate the room without asking anyone for help. As she made her way along the corridor, she saw a few other girls watching her from other parts of the school; she offered a smile to each of them, but she received no smile in return, and by the time she reached the main hallway and saw the huge staircase she couldn't shake the feeling that Holdham Hall seemed like a very unfriendly and unwelcoming place.

"Room thirty, then," she said under her breath, as she began to carry her suitcase up the steps. "I don't suppose that should be too difficult to find."

CHAPTER THREE

1982...

"IT'S AWFULLY BAD OUT there, isn't it?" Sister Lucy said as she followed June into the dark old entrance hallway, which was lit only by the light from several candles on a nearby table. "Rather unwelcoming, I'm afraid."

She looked down at her broken glasses. When she touched the frames, a few stray shards of glass were dislodged from the frames and sent falling onto the tiled floor.

"I really *shall* be in a spot of bother without these," she continued mournfully. "I feel so utterly foolish for dropping them, I know I should be more prepared for this sort of eventuality and I really don't want you to think that I'm some kind of butter-fingered old fool. Honestly, I pride myself on being careful, especially with important things, and now here I've gone and done something foolish when I was so hoping to make a good first impression."

She waited for June to reply.

"This isn't the welcome I was hoping to offer you," she added finally. "However, one mustn't allowed oneself to be distracted just because things are going a little wrong. Sister June, I would like to welcome you to Holdham Hall. Would you care for me to show you around?"

"There'll be no need for that," June said darkly, looking around and then focusing her attention on the large staircase. "I've been here before."

"Blimey, that's a stroke of luck," Lucy replied, stepping over to her. "I've been here for a week now and I'm afraid to say that I haven't really explored the place as fully as I might. There's no electricity, you see. That's why it's so cold in here. You could see your breath if... well, if you could see anything at all." She let out a heavy breath, as if trying to prove her point. "Which you can't. Not really. And of course that means that there's no heating either, so -"

"Why's there no power?" June asked.

"One of those new year problems, I suppose," Lucy said.

"I don't know what that means," June replied, turning to her.

"Neither do I, if I'm honest," Lucy continued. "There's been no power since I arrived. I was told that it would be connected soon, but that doesn't seem to have happened. I can't phone anyone, because... well, again, there's no power. And I was told to await your arrival, so that's what I've been doing while camping out and eating far too much tinned food for my own good. That's how I've been seeing it, really. It's like camping in a really old, really big and rather spooky house."

June watched the stairs for a moment longer, as if she expected to see somebody appear, and then she turned again to the other woman.

"Why?" she asked. "Why are you here at all? Why are either of us here?"

***

"So Holdham Hall closed?" June said a short while later, as she stepped into Mrs. Barker's old office and saw the shelves filled with so many books. "How long ago?"

"Oh, a few decades back now," Lucy

explained, following her through. "I'm afraid I'm not sure of the details, but I was told that the place has been left shuttered for a very long time. I don't mind admitting that it was very dusty when I arrived. I took the liberty of cleaning a few areas, just the parts of the house that I've been using. I expect that if you were to explore the rest of the place, you'd find that it's not in a very good state."

"It hasn't changed much," June replied, heading over to one of the shelves and holding up a candle. She ran a fingertip past the books, disturbing a layer of dust. "It doesn't seem to have changed at all."

"I'm sorry," Lucy continued, "did you say that you were a student here?"

"I'm not sure that's the right word," June said, blowing the dust from her finger before walking over to the desk. "There were some classes, but for the most part Mrs. Barker merely wanted lots of free labor." She looked down at the chair where the old woman used to sit. "Actually, that's not quite fair of me," she added. "We were given enough of an education, certainly for the time. All the girls here had been discarded by their families, or their families had died, so really we were lucky to receive any kind of education at all." She paused, staring at the empty chair. "I should remember that before I'm too ungrateful."

"It seems like a scary place to raise children," Lucy said with a nervous smile. "Did you spend a long time here?"

"Not really," June murmured, "but certainly long enough. And now the First Order has seen fit to send me back after so many years, with no real explanation as to why I'm here."

She looked toward the doorway and saw the hall again.

"But this place has been on my mind lately," she continued. "I saw it in the tunnels beneath the Sahara."

"I'm sorry?" Lucy said. "I don't... quite follow..."

"It's not important," June told her. "At least, I hope it's not. I hope that was just a coincidence and -"

Before she could finish, she heard a bump coming from somewhere upstairs. By the time she looked up at the ceiling, the bump had given way to a set of footsteps running through one of the other rooms. She tried to work out where the footsteps were going, but after a few more seconds the sound faded away to nothing. She waited, and then she turned to Lucy again.

"That has been happening," Lucy told her,

with fear in her eyes. "I was sent here by the First Order to investigate a haunting."

"The First Order?" June said cautiously. "You too?"

Lucy nodded.

"I thought I was the only one," June continued. "The only one from this walk of life, at least."

"I'm usually at St. Clement's in Sussex," Lucy explained eagerly. "Some years ago I was sort of press-ganged into working for the First Order. I've been sent around to a few places, just to investigate odd little happenings here and there. They seem to use me whenever they want to check what's going on in a certain part of the world. I was sent to America, to look into a psychiatric hospital called Lakehurst that was supposedly rather dangerous, but I found that there was nothing to worry about. Then I was sent to an American town called Sobolton, and again, I didn't uncover anything. Then they sent me to a place called Dedston, to look into something about vampires, and then that sort of led me to a Greek island called Thaxos, but that was another dead end. To be honest, I haven't actually uncovered anything unusual until -"

Suddenly they heard the footsteps again, and

Lucy visibly flinched.

"Until now," she added nervously. "I must admit, I *do* think that something rather unusual might be going on here. It's almost as if -"

"Meredith," June whispered.

"I'm sorry?"

"After all these years," June continued, listening as the footsteps faded away once more. "I'm afraid my confidence in coincidences is slipping away rapidly. They must have sent me here for a very good reason. I don't mean to seem self-centered, but I rather fear that has something to do with me."

"With you?"

"With my past," June said, watching the ceiling for a moment longer before turning against to her fellow nun. "With my connection to this place, and the fear I've carried for almost my entire life. I've tried so hard to block it from my mind, I've tried every conceivable way to forget, but nothing has worked for very long and now I'm back. I can only assume that the First Order know exactly what they're doing, in which case they either want me to resolve the mystery of Holdham Hall, or they want to break me in the process."

Hearing more footsteps in the distance, she turned and looked over at the doorway.

"That's three times in as many minutes," Lucy pointed out. "It's never been that frequent before."

"That's because it knows I'm here," June said, as she felt a hardening sense of dread in her chest. "I don't want to sound too full of myself, but I rather fear that it has been waiting for me, ever since the day I was last here. I've hidden the truth, even from myself, but that's not an approach that tends to last for very long. I fear that after so very long, I'm finally going to have to face the one thing that terrified me so much when I was here before... the one thing that very nearly killed me when I was just a little girl."

CHAPTER FOUR

1945...

"IS THIS IT?" JUNE whispered, standing in the doorway and looking into room thirty, where two bare metal beds had been pushed against opposite walls.

One of the beds at least had some sheets laid out, while the other had only a few folded items of linen placed at the bottom next to a sorry-looking pillow. Otherwise the room was bare, save for a thick crack running up one of the walls and extending across the ceiling. The more she looked around, the more June felt that this was less of a bedroom and more of a prison cell. In fact -

"Hello."

Startled, she turned to see another girl

standing behind her.

"You must be June," the girl said, holding out a hand. "Mrs. Barker told me you'd be arriving today. I'm Meredith, and you and I are going to be sharing a room."

"Okay," was all June could say in return, reaching out and shaking the girl's hand, surprised by her cold and somewhat clammy palm. "This is room thirty, isn't it?"

"I know it's not much to look at," Meredith replied, sounding very grown-up as she slipped past and entered the room, "and I can't really think of any way to make it sound better." She stopped and looked around, as if she still couldn't quite believe how awful it looked, and then she turned to June again. "Are your parents dead too?"

June hesitated, surprised by the directness of the question, before nodding.

"No-one here has living parents," Meredith continued. "I suppose if you had living parents, you wouldn't be here in the first place."

"Mummy and Daddy died in the war," June explained. "Daddy was away fighting, and Mummy was in the house when a bomb fell on it. There wasn't anyone left to look after me, so I was sent here. Sometimes I feel very sad about it, but then I remind myself that other people have had worse times."

"My parents both died before the war,"

Meredith said. "I was sent here when I was very young, and I don't really remember anything from before. I don't remember anything about what it's like outside Holdham Hall. I suppose one day I shall get to leave, but Mrs. Barker hasn't told me when that might be. I'm quite scared about leaving, because I don't really know what I'd do out there."

June hesitated, before stepping over to the bed and setting her case down next to the sheets. She wanted to get her few meager possessions out and hang them up as quickly as possible; one thing she particularly disliked was any lack of order.

"You should put that on the floor," Meredith told her. "Mrs. Barker really doesn't like anything put on the beds except sheets and ourselves. I'm sorry, there are so many rules here, it's going to take you a long time to learn them all."

"I'll do my best," June said, moving the case onto the floor and kneeling down before carefully opening the lid. "I wasn't allowed to bring much. They said that I'd be given what I need here."

"That's probably true," Meredith replied mournfully, before looking over her shoulder as if she thought she'd heard someone out in the corridor. She listened for a moment, and then she turned to June again. "I know how things work round here. If you want, I can show you."

***

"There aren't many other children here these days," Meredith explained a short while later, as they made their way back down the stairs. "I don't know why, but now whenever someone leaves, no-one's brought in to take their place. Not often, anyway. You're the first new girl in ages."

"Those pictures are creepy," June said, looking up at the huge paintings that loomed above them from either side. "Who are those people?"

"I don't know," Meredith said, stopping at the top of the last set of steps as three girls walked past the bottom. "That's Alexandra and her friends," she continued, sounding a little dubious. "They think they're in charge here, just because they're older than everyone else."

"Are they mean?" June asked.

"They're horrible," Meredith continued, scrunching her nose up for a moment. "I hate them and I just want them to leave me alone, but they're always pulling these horrible jokes that they think are so funny. Mrs. Barker doesn't even care, she just lets them get away with things."

Suddenly one of the girls at the bottom doubled back and looked up the stairs, evidently having spotted June at the last second.

"Hello, there," Alexandra said with a grin, as her two friends joined her. "You're new, aren't you?"

June nodded.

"It's not often that we get someone new here," Alexandra continued. "Why are you spending your time with Meredith? She's such a stupid thing, you'd be much better off coming with us. You're not actually going to be friends with Meredith, are you?"

"I..."

June hesitated, not quite sure how to respond. She looked at Meredith again and immediately saw the shame in the girl's eyes; she looked at Alexandra, and she saw a kind of bursting over-confidence combined with a grin that somehow seemed to be growing and growing. Behind Alexandra, the other two girls were whispering to one another with what appeared to be ecstatic enjoyment.

"I'm quite alright, thank you," June said finally. "Meredith's just showing me around."

"Well," Alexandra replied, "you don't want to believe everything she tells you. She's got a terrible habit of making things up. Haven't you, Meredith?"

"I don't know," Meredith whimpered, clearly on the verge of tears. "June, it's okay if you want to go and play with them. I understand."

"We'll leave you two to get on with things," Alexandra said, turning and leading her friends away. "Come and find us later, June, when you want to be a bit more popular around here."

Once Alexandra and her two followers were gone, June stood in silence for a moment before turning to see that Meredith still seem cowed. Although she wanted to make her new friend feel better, June had no idea what she could say to help, and a moment later she realized that Meredith was gently sniffing back a few tears.

"It's alright," she said, touching the side of Meredith's arm. "You were going to tell me about the pictures. Remember?"

"It gets scary here at night," Meredith said softly.

"Because of Alexandra?"

Meredith shook her head.

"Then why?" June asked.

"Nobody believes me," Meredith continued, barely able to look June in the eye, "but there's someone else here, someone I don't think anyone else ever sees. It's a woman, and I think..."

Her voice trailed off for a moment.

"What do you think?" June said cautiously.

"You'll think I'm simple in the head."

"I won't," June told her. "I promise."

"She walks around at night," Meredith explained, "going from room to room, almost as if she's searching for something. I don't know what she wants, I only know about her at all because I crept out of my room one night. I told Mrs. Barker and she punished me, she said I was making things up, but I swear I wasn't."

"I believe you," June said. "Have you ever talked to this woman?"

Again, Meredith shook her head.

"Do you know anything else about her?"

Another shake.

"But she scares you, doesn't she?" June continued, picking up on the fear in Meredith's expression. Not just her expression, either; the fear was radiating through her body language. "And no-one's willing to help you, are they?"

"I just get scared at night," Meredith murmured. "Even though I'm in bed and I should be safe, I get scared because... what if the scary woman decides to come and get me? What if she doesn't like the fact that no-one can see her except me?" She sniffed back more tears, but already some had escaped and were trickling down her cheek. "I hope you don't see her," she added finally. "I hope she doesn't *let* you see her."

June thought for a moment, but she knew she had to find some way to make her new friend feel better. The last thing she wanted – the very last thing in the entire world – was to get into any kind of trouble, but she supposed that trouble could be avoided with a dash of cleverness. After a moment, reaching out, she took hold of Meredith's hands and held them tight.

"I think we should find out what's really happening," she told Meredith, forcing a smile that she hoped would soon prove contagious. "I always like solving mysteries, and this seems like a good one. So tonight, after everyone else has gone to bed, we're going to find out who this woman is and where she comes from. And what she wants."

CHAPTER FIVE

1982...

"ARE YOU ABSOLUTELY SURE that we're alone?" June asked as she carried a candle back out into the darkened hallway and looked at the empty staircase. "Are you sure there can't possibly be anyone else in the entire house?"

"Oh, yes," Lucy replied as she hurried after her. "I'm quite -"

Hearing a bump, June turned to see that Lucy had somehow managed to bump straight into the side of the door. Still clutching her broken glasses, and muttering something under her breath, Lucy brushed herself down before making her way over.

"Sorry about that, Sister June. I wasn't

making it up when I said I'm almost blind as a bat without these glasses."

"And you really don't have a spare pair?"

"I know," Lucy sighed. "It's terribly irresponsible of me."

"How long did you say you've been here?"

"Almost a week," Lucy explained. "Perhaps exactly a week. I'm sorry, to be honest my time here has become something of a blur. I've been trying to busy myself by inspecting the place and getting a sense of its history, although it's rather too large for me to make any real inroads." She looked around. "It must have been magnificent when it was in full use, though. I should love to have seen it when it was a school."

"I'm not sure you would," June replied, stepping over to the bottom of the staircase and looking up, spotting the exact place where she had stood with Meredith all those years earlier. She waited, in case the sound of footsteps returned, and then she made her way halfway up before stopping as soon as she saw the landing. "It's cold in here, isn't it?" she continued. "Old Mrs. Barker never much liked paying for heating anyway, but it's particularly cold now." She squinted, but for now the landing was only a dark void at the top of the staircase, although she knew so many corridors and rooms were waiting to be rediscovered. "This seems like a place absolutely fit for ghosts."

"Ghosts?" Lucy replied.

June turned and looked down at her.

"Oh," Lucy continued, "I shouldn't much like to meet a ghost. I've always been under the impression that they're rather nasty things, full of anger and unfinished business." She paused for a moment, still holding her broken glasses. "Do you... I mean, you don't think there could..."

She furrowed her brow.

"I mean, ghosts are a little fanciful, don't you think?" she added. "I'm not saying that I don't believe in them, because I know an awful lot of people think they're real, but it's still rather a lot to get my head around. I suppose I find the whole thing a little freaky, that's all." She looked around again. "I can't imagine what it's like to die, and to be so full of fury and rage that you simply refuse to leave, that you insist on sticking around so that you can try to get some kind of revenge on the people you think wronged you. Why can't these poor souls be left to rest in peace?"

"I don't know what to think," June told her, "but I was sent here by the First Order with no proper instructions, which I can only assume means they think instructions are unnecessary. I suppose they want me to get to the bottom of what happened here, and perhaps even to face my own fears." She looked up toward the landing again. "In the absence of any other business, I shall do precisely that. Not because the First Order wants it, though, and not because of my own fears." She paused, still watching the darkness, waiting in case any kind of shape might start to appear. "I owe it to Meredith. I owe it to her memory."

***

The candle's flickering light picked out a simple plate on the wall, next to the door's jamb, and the number 30 carved into the plate's metal surface.

"Well," June whispered, stopping for a moment as she thought back to the very first time she'd ever seen this room, "here we are again."

Holding the candle out, she looked into the room and saw the same two metal beds that she remembered so well. Meredith's bed was on the left and her own was on the right, and the crack in the wall still ran up and extended across the ceiling. Stepping into the room, June immediately noticed that the air was even colder here, and perhaps thinner too; she could hear herself breathing, and as she looked around she noted that for the most part very little had changed over the intervening decades.

"I'm here, old friend," she said softly. "Are *you* here too?"

She waited, giving Meredith ample time to respond, but she heard only the sound of her own continued breaths. She wasn't even sure exactly what she'd been expecting, save that she'd perhaps thought Meredith's ghostly figure might appear to welcome her back to Holdham Hall; she knew now that this had been a foolish idea, an almost cartoonish and certainly grotesque mockery of the truth, and as she turned and looked all around the room she wondered whether Meredith's ghost might instead be hiding.

Finally she stopped as she saw a figure standing in the doorway.

"Room thirty?" Lucy said, still holding her glasses. "Is this... significant in some way?"

"It was," June admitted.

"There are lots of rooms like this," Lucy continued, taking a step forward. "They're all pretty much identical, in fact. Well, apart from that crack. I don't recall having seen that before."

"It was always here," June told her, turning to look at the crack as she felt a sense of dread starting to fill her chest.

"Are you sure?"

"Yes," June replied.

"Are you *really* sure? I feel certain that I would have noticed something like that."

"I do not wish to disagree with you," June said, keeping her eyes fixed on the crack, "but on this matter I must respectfully insist that I am correct. That crack was most certainly here thirty-seven years ago, when I first set foot in Holdham Hall."

"Well, I suppose you're probably right," Lucy muttered. "I've never been particularly observant. That's always been one of my many failings."

June hesitated, struggling to really pay too much attention to Lucy's words as she continued to stare at the crack. Having put so many memories to the back of her mind for so long, she now found that many of them were starting to wriggle back through to the front of her thoughts, and after a moment she took a step forward before stopping herself. She'd been about to disturb another element of the past, although at the back of her mind she couldn't help but wonder whether she was making a terrible mistake. After all, the First Order might have directed her back to Holdham Hall, but did that mean that she had to do their bidding?

"I can't imagine all the poor little children living in this place," Lucy said airily. "Don't get me wrong, I'm sure they were well looked after, but it doesn't seem like a very... inspiring place."

"It wasn't," June murmured, still watching the crack.

"And you said you were one of them, I believe?" Lucy continued. "I bet you're glad you grew up and got away. Oh, I do hope that being here again after so long doesn't bring back any bad memories. It doesn't, does it?"

"One cannot live without remembering the past," June observed, finding now that she was unable to look away from the crack on the wall. "If one tries, one won't get very far."

"Still, it must be unfortunate to find yourself here again," Lucy suggested. "You know, sometimes I wonder why the First Order have to be so mysterious all the time. Once they sent me into the wilderness in America hunting for some town called Devil's Briar. I never found the place, and I'm pretty certain it never existed at all, but they had me going round and round in circles on a hunt. It reminded me of a visit I had to pay to a village called Cobblefield, where..."

As Lucy's continued to talk, June finally stepped forward. Finding now that she was able to ignore the other woman's drone, she turned her head and placed an ear against the crack, and now Lucy's babbling voice seemed further away than ever. Instead June heard the silence inside the crack, a silence that she remembered from many years earlier; she leaned a little closer, until her ear gently touched the cold crumbling plaster on either side of the crack in the wall, and after a few more seconds June realized that she was inadvertently holding her breath.

"Hello?" she whispered. "Is anyone there?"

CHAPTER SIX

1945...

"HELLO?" MEREDITH WHISPERED, WITH her ear pressed against the crack in the bedroom wall. "Can anyone hear me?"

"What are you doing?" June asked.

Startled, Meredith spun round to see that June had returned a little early from the communal bathroom. A few other girls were laughing as they walked past on the way to their own rooms.

"Nothing," Meredith said cautiously, before realizing that she'd been caught red-handed and couldn't really talk her way out of the awkward situation. "Sometimes I hear the ghost talking to me through the crack."

June stared at her, as if she couldn't quite

believe what she was hearing.

"That's the look," Meredith continued, sitting on the end of her bed and putting her hands over her face. "I get it from everyone. They all think I'm crazy."

"I don't think you're crazy," June said, making her way over and sitting next to her, then putting an arm around her new friend. "What does the ghost say to you when it talks through the crack?"

"It whispers mean things," Meredith explained. "It tells me that it's going to get me."

"I see," June continued, "but it never actually *does* come to get you, does it?"

"Not yet."

"That seems like a very strange thing for a ghost to threaten," June pointed out. "I'd have thought that when a ghost wants to get you, it'd just come and do whatever it wants."

"That's what I thought too," Meredith replied, "but I don't think it works like that."

"Hmm," June said, looking over at the crack again, her mind whirring as she tried to make sense of everything that was happening. "I don't really have any experience with ghosts, but I don't think there's any point hiding from what's happening. You told me that this ghost walks around downstairs, and I think we should go and try to see it."

"What if it hurts us?"

"It hasn't so far," June reminded her, before squeezing her tight in an attempt to make her feel a little braver. "And before there was just you, but now I'm going to be here to help you. There are two of us, and only one of the ghost. We'll wait until everyone else has gone to sleep, and then we'll sneak downstairs, and we'll make sure that Mrs. Barker doesn't catch us. How does that sound?"

"Okay," Meredith said cautiously, although she was clearly terrified. "Thank you, June. Somehow now that you're here, I feel like everything's going to be alright."

***

The grand entrance hallway of Holdham Hall stood bathed in moonlight that shone through the large stained-glass windows. The hallway had been silent for some time now, since everyone had retired for bed, but finally this silence was broken by the sound of two young girls making their way slowly and carefully down the staircase.

"I don't hear anyone," Meredith whispered as they reached the bottom of the stairs. "It's really cold, though."

"Where do you see the ghost?" June asked, looking all around.

"The dining room," Meredith replied.

June hesitated, before taking hold of

Meredith's hand and leading her through toward the dining room, where the long table stood with empty chairs on either side.

"Do you see those windows?" Meredith asked.

June turned and saw six large, tall windows running along the wall.

"She goes to the one at the end," Meredith continued. "Always. She goes and stands at the sixth window and she looks outside."

"And then what?" June asked.

"I don't know," Meredith admitted. "To be honest, I always get too scared and I run away."

"Are you scared now?" June replied, squeezing her hand a little tighter. "I'm here, so at least you're not alone."

"I know," Meredith said, "but -"

Suddenly she looked past June, as if she'd heard something.

"What is it?" June whispered.

"I'm not sure," Meredith said, watching the open doorway they'd both passed through just a moment earlier, "but I think I might have..."

June waited for her to continue. She hadn't heard anything herself, but she could tell with absolute certainty that Meredith wasn't making up stories. A strange kind of non-silence hung in the air, as if June could feel that a noise was about to ring out through the room, yet as the seconds ticked past she heard no such thing. She opened her mouth to ask whether Meredith was sure, but as she continued to watch the doorway she realized that she was now absolutely expecting a ghostly figure to appear.

"There!" Meredith hissed. "Do you hear?"

"Hear what?" June replied.

"Her footsteps! They're coming this way!"

"I don't hear any footsteps," June said, "but -"

"Hurry!" Meredith said, pulling her down onto the floor and then forcing her to follow as she crawled under the table, finding a spot between the chair legs. "She's here!"

"Where?" June asked, looking around but only seeing the various wooden legs on every side. "I don't see anything."

"She's so close now," Meredith continued, peering out toward the doorway. "This is how it always goes, she comes closer and closer until it seems she must be here, and then -"

Suddenly she let out a gasp and pulled back, bumping one of the chairs in the process and causing its legs to scrape against the floor.

"I don't see her," June said, keeping her voice as low as possible.

"There!" Meredith mouthed, pointing past her.

June turned to look, but she saw absolutely

no sign of anyone. She waited in case her eyes needed time to adjust, yet still she saw only the chair legs and – further off – the far side of the room bathed in moonlight from the six windows. Blinking, she wondered how she could be missing whatever had terrified Meredith, but when she looked over at her friend she saw absolute pure terror written all over the girl's face. Slowly, Meredith began to turn her head, as if she was watching the slow progress of someone walking past the table.

"What do you see?" June asked, looking again across the room.

Meredith pointed more frantically this time, yet still June saw nothing.

"There's nothing there," June continued, unable to hide a sense of frustration that was starting to fill her voice. "Are you sure you're not just seeing a shadow?"

"She's right over there," Meredith whispered, pointing now toward the sixth window. "It's just like I told you! She's standing at that window and looking out."

June stared at that particular window, yet still she saw nothing untoward. Feeling a growing sense of frustration starting to rise through her chest, she found herself torn between two possibilities: either she was somehow unable to see this ghostly apparition, or there was no apparition and the whole thing existed only in Meredith's mind. She continued to watch the window, fully open to the idea that the ghost might appear at any moment, but of the two possibilities it was the latter now that seemed to be moving more and more to the forefront.

"What does she want?" Meredith asked quietly.

"Tell me exactly what she looks like," June replied.

"She's wearing an old gown," Meredith continued, "that goes all the way to the floor, covering her feet. She has long black hair that hangs almost all the way down her back. Her eyes are like two black marbles, and she's very thin, and when she opens her mouth she has horrid dirty teeth. But why are you asking? Can't you see her for yourself?"

"I'm trying," June told her.

"I can't look!" Meredith said, putting her hands over her eyes. "It's too awful!"

"I still don't see her," June said, craning her neck now to get a better look at the sixth window, but still seeing nothing unusual. "Meredith, I really don't mean to doubt you, but I truly believe that we're alone at least now." She turned to see that Meredith still had her hands covering her eyes. "Come on," she continued with a faint sigh, "there's no need to be so scared. I'm right here with you and

I won't let anything bad happen."

As those last words left her lips, June was surprised to realize that she sounded so grown-up.

Slowly Meredith lowered her hands and looked out toward the window.

"She's gone," she whispered. "Where did she go?"

"Are you really sure she was here at all?" June asked. "I don't mean to suggest that you were wrong, but I have to insist again that I didn't see anyone at all." She watched the side of Meredith's face, still trying to work out what was going on in the girl's mind. "Do you think perhaps we should go back up to our room before we're caught? I'd hate to get into trouble on my very first night here at Holdham Hall."

"I..."

Meredith continued to watch the window for a moment, before slowly turning to June. She opened her mouth to say something, but at the last second she froze as if suddenly shocked by something in her field of vision.

"Behind you!" she gasped. "June... I can see her again! She's found us! She's right behind you!"

CHAPTER SEVEN

1982...

"NO?" JUNE SAID AFTER a moment, pulling back from the crack in the bedroom wall. "Not now? Or not yet? Or perhaps never?"

"Are you... talking to the wall?" Lucy asked.

"I suppose I am," June muttered, feeling as if perhaps she was on a hiding to nothing. Turning to Lucy, she realized that she hadn't explained herself very well. "It was just an idea, that's all. A foolish notion, you might say, that something from a long time ago might repeat itself. Something that, if I'm being completely honest, most likely never even happened in the first place."

"I see," Lucy said, clearly still puzzled. "I mean... I don't see, actually. You'll have to forgive me, Sister June, but I'm feeling rather lost."

"I think..."

June hesitated, before slowly turning to her.

"Thirty-seven years might not seem like a long time," she explained after a moment, "and in some regards indeed it is not. But in the life of a human being, it can be an age. I have always preferred not to think about myself too much, not to become too self-centered, but in this particular case I fear I must look back at my own past. When I was last at this house, something happened that I tried very hard to forget, but since then I have grown up and I have... experienced certain things. I now return to the house with an entirely new perspective, one that makes me wonder whether I was correct all those years ago."

She looked around for a moment before turning to Lucy again.

"What have you heard since you arrived here last week?" she asked.

"Well, I... I have heard footsteps," Lucy admitted.

"Coming from nowhere? As if unattached to any living soul?"

"That is certainly how it has seemed to me. At first I thought it might be down to some natural phenomenon, like a mouse perhaps." She paused, as if even as those words left her lips she knew they were unlikely to convince anyone. "A mouse wearing rather large shoes?"

"But have you *seen* anything untoward?"

"No," Lucy replied, shaking her head slightly. "At least... I don't think so."

"Oh, you'd know if you had," June told her. "If you saw what Meredith claimed to have seen all those years ago, you'd be absolutely terrified."

"I'd certainly remember that," Lucy said somewhat sheepishly.

"And you've heard nothing else? No voices?"

"I'm sorry."

"Don't be sorry," June continued, trying to organize her thoughts in some frantic attempt to resolve the mystery in an instant. "The footsteps sounded hurried, though, did they not? They certainly didn't sound to me like the footsteps of some terrifying spectral vision."

"No, I suppose not."

"But I don't want to consider what that might ultimately mean," June said, heading to the doorway and looking out into the corridor, then turning to look back over at the crack in the wall. "I want you to stay here, Sister Lucy," he added, "and I know how strange this will seem, but I want you to listen to that crack."

"Listen to it?"

"Put your ear to it."

"Why?"

"Because I intend to test a hypothesis," June told her, still assembling the fragments of thought into what she hoped might become a cohesive theory. "It's a hypothesis I should have considered all those years ago."

***

Having returned alone to the grand old dining room, June made her way past the large table, stopping at the end and turning to look down at the wooden surface. For a moment she remembered how it had felt to hide under there with Meredith, and how -

No.

No, she knew this was not the right moment to engage in nostalgia.

Instead, she made her way past the windows until she reached the one at the far end. The sixth window, on first inspection, seemed no different to the other five; all these windows were wide and tall, and decorated with the most astonishing stained glass art that June had ever seen in her life. Now, in the darkness and with only a single candle for illumination, this stained glass appeared rather dull, but June knew full well that in the morning light it positively shone with bright colors. She looked up at the glass now, remembering her own attempts to make such decorations as a young woman and recalling the dismal results; she had gained a new respect for stained glass over time, recognizing it as one of the truest art forms in the world, a kind of merging of the natural and artificial worlds to create something truly wondrous.

Moving the thick, dusty curtain aside, she saw something that she dimly remembered from her childhood, something that she had mostly ignored at the time: another crack in the wall.

She hesitated, before leaning closer and listening to this crack. When this produced no remarkable results, she turned and moved her lips closer. The idea she was about to test still seemed preposterous in every regard, yet she had learned since her trip to Switzerland that sometimes the preposterous could be used to explain the mundane.

"Hello?" she said finally, before realizing that she needed to raise her voice a little louder. "Hello?" she said again. "Can anybody hear me?"

She waited, still half-convinced that she was on a fool's errand.

"Hello?" a voice replied suddenly, sounding rather bemused as it emerged from the crack. "Is that... Sister June, is that you?"

"Hello, Sister Lucy," June continued. "You're coming across loud and clear."

"As are you," Lucy said, "but... I don't quite understand what's going on."

"We're a long way apart in this dark old building," June pointed out, "but somehow our voices carry perfectly through this crack." She looked up, seeing that the crack ran its way all the way up to the top of the wall. "This must be a one-in-a-million chance, but I believe that the acoustics of the building permit this to happen. Somehow voices carry with remarkable fidelity from room thirty up there, all the way down here to the dining room." She looked at the stained glass again. "To this very spot, right next to the sixth window."

"How is that possible?" Lucy asked.

"Oh, some combination of acoustics and... I don't entirely know, but I'm sure there's some dry theory that would explain it all, if one were to consult an expert on such matters. Which we don't have time to do at this precise moment." She ran a fingertip against the crack, feeling its rough edges and trying to imagine how such a fissure could possibly run all the way up to the bedroom near the top of the building. "Is that what Meredith would have heard?" she mused. "All that time, sleeping in her bed next to the crack, and she might have been subconsciously listening to whatever was happening right down here at this window."

"What was that?" Lucy called out through the crack, clearly raising her voice in an attempt to be heard better. "Sorry, Sister June, but you're becoming a little mumbled!"

"It's nothing!" June replied loudly. "Would you mind popping down to join me? I think I might be onto something, but I'm probably going to require your assistance. Would that be alright?"

"Of course!" Lucy shouted back. "I'll be right down." She paused for a moment. "Uh... over and out!"

"Over and out, indeed," June said, staring at the crack again as she thought once more of Meredith sleeping all that time ago in her bed. "Where you hearing something being whispered?" she continued. "Forget about what happened when you were awake, that might be entirely inconsequential. When you were asleep and dreaming, Meredith, were you hearing the whispers of a ghost all the way down here at the sixth window? And if you were, what was that ghost telling you?"

Hearing footsteps, she turned to see Lucy making her way back into the room.

"That was quick," June pointed out, furrowing her brow.

"Well, I hurried," Lucy explained with a smile, sounding a little out of breath as she fiddled yet again with her broken glasses. "I didn't want to be tardy. You seemed like you were in a hurry."

"I suppose I did," June admitted, still struggling to understand how anyone could possibly have made their way down from the bedrooms all the way to the dining room so quickly. After a few seconds, she realized that there was perhaps no need to dwell on that mystery; like the acoustics of the crack in the wall, there was most likely a perfectly reasonable explanation that would take far too much time to figure out. "This school has been shut for quite some time," she continued, "but it appears that none of the furniture was ever taken away."

"Apparently not," Lucy agreed.

"In which case," June added, "might the old school records still be around somewhere? There's something I need to check."

CHAPTER EIGHT

1945...

"GET OUT FROM UNDER there at once!" Mrs. Barker snarled, grabbing June's arm and hauling her out from under the dining table, forcing her to stand. "What in the name of all that's holy are you two reprehensible children doing?"

"I'm sorry!" June gasped. "We only -"

Before she could finish, Mrs. Barker slapped her hard on the side of the face, before turning and yanking Meredith out from under the table as well.

"I've never known such abysmal behavior," Mrs. Barker continued, looking at each of them in turn as if she genuinely couldn't believe what was happening. "I expect discipline and good behavior from the girls in my school and I will not tolerate deception in any form!"

"We're sorry," June said, "but -"

"No excuses!" Mrs. Barker screamed at the top of her voice. "Excuses are for Satan! What I want from you two is some proper behavior, and instead I find you sneaking around in the middle of the night like a pair of utter hooligans! It's clear, Meredith, that your time here so far has been entirely wasted and you're going to have to be reminded of your duties and responsibilities!" She turned to June. "As for you, young lady, evidently your parents – dead though they are – deserve condemnation for failing to raise you properly!"

Still holding each girl by the wrist, she half led and half dragged them toward the door.

"There is a plague in this country," she continued as she forced them into the hallway, "of bad parenting. When any fool can produce children, with no training or qualifications whatsoever, the result is a generation of badly-raised brats who will become equally badly-behaving adults, who will in turn raised another generation of idiots. We might have won the war against Nazi Germany, but we are entering into a battle against a league of homegrown horrors that over the decades might grow to become just as great a threat."

"You're hurting me!" Meredith sobbed.

June opened her mouth to say the same,

before deciding to hold back at the last moment. After all, she hated the idea of giving Mrs. Barker any satisfaction.

"Well," the woman continued, "if you're too alert to sleep, then I'm just going to have to find some way to tire your recalcitrant little minds. Fortunately, I have two rather scuffed floors that are in need of a good clean!"

"I want to go to bed!" Meredith protested. "I'm so tired!"

"Well, you should have thought of that before you decided to be so disobedient," Mrs. Barker snapped. "There are fifty-three girls in this school, and fifty-one of them are tucked up in their beds, doing the right thing by sleeping and restoring their energies so that they're ready for the next day. You two are the only ones who seem unable and unwilling to conform, and that approach to life might have worked for you so far, but I'm afraid you've run into the one thing that's going to beat such insubordination out of you." She looked down and glared at them both. "Me!"

***

On her hands and knees in one of the other halls at the far end of the house, June dipped the rag into a nearby bucket of dirty soapy water and then got back to work cleaning the tiles. She shifted the weight on her knees a little, trying to find some respite from the pain, but deep down she knew that she was never going to get comfortable.

Looking up, she saw that she was perhaps a third of the way across the room now, and she supposed that with a little luck and perseverance she might be done by the time the sun came up.

A moment later, hearing a distant sobbing sound, she turned and looked over at a nearby door. She and Meredith had been separated and set to work in different rooms, with clear instructions that they weren't to talk, but now June felt desperately sorry for her new friend. She knew Mrs. Barker had returned to her room upstairs, so after a few seconds she got to her feet – feeling an immediately lessening of the pain in her knees – she headed across the room. When she looked through the doorway, she saw that Meredith had stopped working and was merely weeping on the floor.

"It's okay," June said, stepping into the room and heading over, then crouching down to put a hand on the other girl's shoulder. "We won't be here forever."

"That's easy for you to say," Meredith whimpered.

"No, I mean it," June continued. "We're the same age, aren't we? In a few years from now, we'll be sent off somewhere else, and I'm sure things will be better. After all, nowhere can be as bad as

Holdham Hall, can it?"

"What if it's worse?"

"I can't imagine what that would be like."

"The older girls usually get sent to live with families in London or Birmingham," Meredith told her. "Occasionally one gets picked to go and join some nuns instead. I don't want to live in London or Birmingham, and I definitely don't want to be a nun."

"I agree," June said with a sigh, "but there might be other options."

"Like what?"

"Well, I'm not entirely sure," June admitted, "but the important thing to remember is that we won't always be here at this horrible place, with its dusty old rooms and dull floors." She looked around the room for a moment. "Actually, that's not fair of me, is it? I'm sure the house is perfectly splendid, it's just that the school is run by... well, perhaps Mrs. Barker has her reasons. I suppose she's right that we could use a spot of discipline."

"I hate her," Meredith said through gritted teeth, as tears glistened on her cheeks.

"Hate is a horrible and much over-used word," June told her.

"Sometimes you don't talk like we're the same age," Meredith replied. "You sound older."

"My parents believed that a child should be involved in conversations," June explained. "They encouraged me to speak to them about whatever was on my mind, and I suppose I learned to be more articulate."

"What does that mean?"

"It means that one can defend whatever one believes," June told her. "Listen, Mrs. Barker expects us to have these floors done in the morning, but part of me thinks that she'd enjoy coming down and finding that we've failed. She'd probably get all up on her high horse again, stomping about and giving us more punishments. But can you imagine her face if she comes down and finds that we've done a magnificent job?"

"It's too much hard work," Meredith told her.

"Not for the end result," June said with a faint smile, "which would be to show her that we're not as bad as she thinks." She waited, hoping that her words might galvanize Meredith and spur her to get back to work, but after a few seconds she realized that she was perhaps going to have to try another approach. "Well, I for once intend to prove her wrong, so I'm going to work twice as hard and four times as fast." Getting to her feet, she took a step back. "You do what you can, Meredith, and then I'll come through and help you out in this room. We'll get it all done just so long as we work as a team."

Again she waited, but Meredith seemed

utterly defeated, as if she couldn't possibly rouse herself to get back to work.

"There's no point feeling sorry for ourselves," June said, hauling herself up and heading back to the other room, feeling exhausted but also determined to prove Mrs. Barker wrong. "Nobody ever got much done by sitting around and feeling sorry for themselves, did they?"

Reaching the doorway, and realizing that Meredith hadn't replied, she stopped and looked back. She saw that her new friend hadn't moved at all and was still sitting doing nothing; for a fraction of a second June felt a little irritated, before reminding herself that Meredith had spent much longer at Holdham Hall and had evidently been more fully broken down by the experience. In that moment June told herself that she was never going to let the same thing happen to her own spirit, that she was going to find a way to navigate the challenges of the school without giving in or letting her own soul suffer. If that meant working extra hard, then she'd just work extra hard.

"It's going to be okay," she said finally. "One day we're going to be far away from here, we're going to be grown-ups Meredith and we're going to laugh about our time here at this horrible old place. I promise."

CHAPTER NINE

1982...

"I ALWAYS KNEW THAT old Mrs. Barker would keep good records," June said, tilting the latest folder so that she could reach the title by candlelight. "She seemed like such a stickler for bureaucracy and paperwork."

"What are you hoping to find?" Lucy asked, glancing around the office. "I must admit, I didn't come in here very often until now. I thought this seemed like a rather spooky part of the house. Of course, there's the main hall a little further off. I haven't been in there at all. Not yet."

"There seems to be a record in here for every child who ever came to Holdham Hall," June explained. "I was hoping that they'd be arranged alphabetically, but for some reason they seem to be arranged based on the rooms they occupied, which is making it a little more difficult to locate the records I'm after." She set the folder aside and picked up another, squinting in an attempt to read the spidery handwriting. "She seems to have kept the records herself. I always noticed that she seemed very reluctant to accept help from anyone else. Aside from a few teaching assistants, she ran the entire school as almost a one-woman band."

She looked at another folder, then another, before finally holding up one that had a small photo of Meredith attached.

"Who's that?" Lucy asked.

"Someone who has been gone for a long time now," June said, her voice pregnant with emotion as she moved the candle a little closer so that she could see better. "Her name was Meredith, and she was the first – well, the only – friend I made when I came here."

"She looks nice."

"She was a sweet child," June replied as she began to leaf through the folder. "I'm afraid I didn't know her for very long before she..."

Her voice trailed off as she reached the end of the file.

"Before she what?" Lucy said after a moment.

"There's really nothing of any great

importance in here," June said, before holding up another folder and reading the name under the photo. "Judith Culver." She held up another folder. "Wendy Wickerstaff. These are the two girls who were in room thirty before Meredith moved in."

"They look nice too."

"The dates, though," June continued, "are something of a surprise. Do you see?"

"It's hard to read the writing."

"They both died young," June said, as she started checking some more folders. "And the same here. But not this one. This one again." She rifled through several more folders before setting them down. "Exactly half the girls who stayed in room thirty died before they could leave the school."

"Half?" Lucy replied. "Why would something make half of them die?"

"Because they slept in that bed," June whispered. "There's no record of which bed each girl used, of course, but I'd wager that we can guess. If I'm right, ever girl who slept on the bed next to the crack in the wall was dead within..." She took another look at a couple of the folders. "Within a few months," she added. "Only Meredith lasted longer than six months, and that was only by a matter of weeks."

"Why would the bed kill them?"

"The bed had nothing to do with it," June said, "except for its positioning." She turned to

Lucy as the candle flickered, casting a dancing line of light across one side of her face. "Each of those girls must have heard the whisper from downstairs while they slept. And whatever that voice was saying... it must have been fatal. I remember hearing rumors about something happening, something connected to that room, but I thought it was just the usual childish nonsense. Now I'm not so sure."

***

"You're going to think that I'm a rather silly fool," Lucy said as she followed June through into Mrs. Barker's old office, "but I'm afraid I haven't quite connected the dots here. Who was whispering what into the crack in the wall?"

"That's only one of the questions I'm struggling with," June replied as she headed to the desk and stopped to look down at the old books that had been left in place. "Right now, I'm also wondering why the First Order sent me here. Any idea of a coincidence has completely gone away, it's almost as if..."

She looked around, as if troubled by something else in the room.

"Nothing has changed," she added finally.

"You pointed that out before," Lucy reminded her.

"Yes, but *nothing* has changed," June continued. "It's exactly how it was when I left many years ago. I'm sure something must have changed in the time between that day and the school's closure, but as I stand here today and look all around I can see that it's all exactly the same. Is it possible that the First Order is behind that?"

"Why would we... ever think that?" Lucy asked, before shaking her head. "I'm sorry, I just don't... I can't quite understand what you're driving at."

"They sent me here tonight," June said, with a hint of foreboding in her voice. "I was in Africa, they brought me home and they told me they had a new mission for me. I was picked up at the airport, and then something caused a delay and I was kept in a hotel for a few weeks. Now, mere days into the new year, I've been dropped off here at Holdham Hall with some vague instructions to stay until I'm told to leave again." She paused for a moment. "They must know what happened to me here. Meredith, Mrs. Barker, the other children... I'm quite sure that the First Order will know everything about my life from the moment I arrived to the moment I was taken to the convent. The question is, why did they sent me here? And why *now*, of all times?"

"What do you think the explanation could be?" Lucy asked.

"They know that this mystery was never solved," June explained ."They know that no-one ever worked out why Meredith died, and I suppose the same question stands for the other girls in that bed as well."

"So they want you to solve it?" Lucy suggested. "I've been sent around the world by the First Order too, you know. They sent me to London to investigate a werewolf named Duncan, who I never found. They sent me to Norway to hunt for ghosts on a farm, but there were no ghosts, at least not as far as I could determine. One time I was even sent to the jungle to find a tomb that some said didn't even exist. Of course, I couldn't find it either. To be honest, they sent me here, there and everywhere, but I never uncover anything of interest. Sometimes I feel like something of a failure."

"Why would the First Order care about a simple ghost story?" June mused.

"I don't know," Lucy replied. "Why would they?"

"They wouldn't," June said, stepping around from behind the desk as she felt a growing sense of concern in the back of her mind. "I'm sure their files are filled with ghost stories. One more wouldn't make much difference, unless..."

Her voice trailed off for a few seconds.

"Unless this time I'm the subject," she

continued finally, "and *I'm* the one being studied, in which case I wonder, would they trust me to observe myself? Would they let me report on my own case? Or would they..."

She hesitated, looking across the room, before slowly turning to Lucy.

"Or would they send someone else to do that part?"

"Hmm?" Lucy replied innocently. "I beg your pardon?"

"What did they ask you to do here, exactly?" June continued.

"They were rather vague," Lucy told her, although she seemed a little uncomfortable now. "It was the usual stuff, really. I'm to write up a report about anything unusual that happens. As I mentioned before, I tend never to find very much of interest. Deep down, I fear that I might be considered to be something of a failure in this regard. I often wonder why they send me to investigate things at all, and I've always just assumed that they're short-handed."

"Have you ever met a bear?" June asked.

"A bear?"

"This particular bear can turn into a man."

"Like a... bear-wolf?"

"I think the term is were-bear."

"Oh. No, I haven't. Why do you ask?"

"Forget it," June said, shaking her head,

"that might be a coincidence too far." She looked Lucy up and down for a moment, noting the details of her habit. "A similarity too far, indeed. What convent are you from? I'm sure you mentioned it, but I'm afraid I mustn't have been paying attention."

"St. Wendy's," Lucy told her. "It's up north, I often find that not many people have heard of it. It's rather small, you see, and not nearly as glamorous as more other places."

"I see," June said, before letting out a sigh. "I don't know about you, Sister Lucy, but I'm awfully tired. I think perhaps I might like to get an hour or two of sleep, just so that I'm able to tackle this matter more fully in the morning and give it my full attention."

"Absolutely," Lucy replied, and then she paused for a few seconds. "Where are you going to do that, though?"

"Where else?" June said. "For the sake of old times, I rather think I should take my old place up in room thirty."

CHAPTER TEN

1945...

"WHY ARE YOU SITTING there all alone like that?"

Startled, having been lost in thought all morning, June turned to see that Alexandra and two other girls had made their way over to join her at the far end of the garden, away from the house itself.

"Haven't you got any friends?" Alexandra asked. "Oh! Wait, I saw you with Meredith yesterday, but does she really count as a friend? I mean, she's rather silly, isn't she? She's a flimsy, weak sort of person."

"She seems rather pleasant to me," June replied, bristling slightly at Alexandra's rudeness.

"She has been perfectly kind and hospitable to me."

"It's okay," Alexandra continued, "you're new here so you can be forgiven a kind of rookie mistake. It's natural for you to try to fall in with the first person who shows you a little attention, but you'll soon realize that you have some much better options." She stepped over and sat next to June, while her two associates hung back a little. "If you want to do well here," she continued, "you need to stick with the right group."

"And what would be the right group?" June asked.

"I know how old Barker works," Alexandra informed her. "I know how to get whatever I want in this place, with very little effort. Barker's not immune to flattery, you see, and she'll be kind to you if you become one of her favorites. I'm her absolute most favorite of all, so I can get away with absolutely anything. Adults aren't really that different to the rest of us, not once you've learned how to manipulate them."

"I'm not sure that I want to manipulate anyone," June countered.

"You won't get very far with that attitude," Alexandra chuckled, patting her hard on the back. "Holdham Hall's about survival, more than anything else. Look at me, for example, I'm going to be out of here soon. I managed to annoy the nuns so that they wouldn't pick me, so I'll be moving to London, and when I get there I'm going to start making a name for myself. Sure, I'll have to work as a cook or a maid for a little while, but I'm going to find myself a nice man and have him take care of me. As I said, it's all about manipulating people to get what you want from them."

"That sounds somewhat... mercenary," June suggested.

"I don't care," Alexandra replied, patting her on the back again. "What's the alternative? A life of drudgery? No thanks!" She got to her feet and stepped back over to her friends, before turning to June. "Once I've left this place, I daresay I'll soon forget it even exists. Just make sure you make it out alive, though, because it'd be awful if you became the next victim of the ghost."

"What ghost?" June asked.

"Look over there," Alexandra said, pointing at the house. "Do you see the stained glass windows of the dining hall?"

"Yes, but -"

"Look at the sixth window along," Alexandra continued. "There's a clear panel at the bottom, it's the only one you can even slightly see through. There's a ghostly woman who looks out at the world from that panel, at least that's what I've heard."

"Have you seen her yourself?" June replied, keen to downplay the idea entirely.

"Don't be stupid," Alexandra said as June turned to her. "How could I have seen her? Everyone knows the story of what happens here. If you see the ghost at the sixth window, you're not long for this world. Every single girl who's ever seen her has died almost immediately."

June turned to her.

"Actually," Alexandra continued with a keen grin, "most of them have been sleeping in room thirty. Maybe even all of them. In fact, if you ask me, anyone who sleeps in room thirty is cursed!"

"Do you seriously expect me to believe that?" June asked.

"Believe what you want," Alexandra said, as she and her friends turned to walk away. "You might want to reconsider who you spend your time with, though. You're in for a tough few years here if you insist on trying to be friends with idiots like Meredith."

***

A few minutes later, having made her way past the other girls playing and chatting on the lawn, June approached the windows that overlooked the dining room. Standing on the grass, she had to stand on tiptoes to get a better look at the stained glass of the sixth window, but as she peered at the panel in the corner she was relieved to see no sign of anyone staring out at her from the other side.

"That settles that, then," she whispered under her breath, although she couldn't entirely forget Alexandra's mocking words.

"If you see the ghost at the sixth window," the other girl's voice explained, echoing in June's mind, "you're not long for this world. Every single girl who's ever seen her has died almost immediately."

"What are you doing over here?" Mrs. Barker asked, and June turned to see her storming closer.

"Nothing," June stammered, "I just -"

"I won't have you causing trouble like this."

"I wasn't causing trouble!" June protested, before realizing that she perhaps needed to moderate her tone. "I'm sorry, Mrs. Barker," she continued, glancing around and seeing that all the other girls were getting along with each other. "You're right, I should talk to people more."

"I've got my eye on you, you know," Mrs. Barker said firmly. "You haven't been here for very long, June, but already I sense you're going to cause me a lot of trouble. Am I right in that assessment?"

"No!" June replied quickly. "I mean... I certainly will try not to."

"I don't want you to try. I want it to come naturally."

"Yes, Mrs. Barker."

June waited, but for a few seconds the headmistress merely glared at her.

"But you have potential," Mrs. Barker opined finally. "Not much, but some. That's what I find most frustrating about you. Every year, the good sisters of St. Jude's come to this school and select one girl to go and live with them. It's the highest accolade any girl here can earn, it's a true honor, and they set great stock in my recommendations. If I tell them that a girl is likely to do well with them, that girl is almost guaranteed to be chosen. Would you like that sort of life, June?"

"I... don't know," June said cautiously.

"Did your parents take you to church?"

"Of course!"

"And did you go willingly, or did you have to be dragged?"

"I think I went willingly," June told her.

"Do you have faith in the Lord?"

"Faith?" June had to think about that question for a moment. "I don't know," she admitted cautiously. "I'd like to think so."

"It's not a trick question," Mrs. Barker said, rolling her eyes. "Either you do, or you don't." She sighed heavily, before grabbing June by the arm and leading her toward the other girls. "You mustn't think too much, June. Thinking will get you into a great deal of trouble. As I tell the girls in my glasses, you're all here to be told things, and if you think and ask questions you'll show that process down. Why, if I could ban you all from talking, I think I would!"

"Yes, Mrs. Barker," June said sheepishly. "Where's Meredith?"

"I don't know where that scrawny little girl has got to, but I'm sure I'll be disappointed when I find out. Now, I saw you talking to Alexandra earlier. She's a good example of how you should behave here." Stopping, she forced June to turn to her. "As I told you, you have potential. Not much, but some. Try to live up to that."

"Mrs. Barker," June replied, "might I ask just one question?"

"What is it?"

"I heard a story about the window," June explained. "The sixth window. Is it true that -"

"Let me stop you there," Mrs. Barker snarled, clearly angry at the merest mention of any such tale. "Do not indulge in foolishness, June. Young minds have a tendency to listen to such ideas without question, and you won't get very far if you do the same. There is no such thing as ghosts, and there is certainly no ghost at that window. From now on, I want you to understand that any girl who speaks of such nonsense will suffer thirty lashes across my desk. Am I being clear enough for you?"

June opened her mouth to ask another

question, but she managed to stop herself at the very last second.

"Yes, Mrs. Barker," she managed finally. "I'm sorry, Mrs. Barker."

"Now mingle with the other girls before I call you in for your first class of the day," Mrs. Barker replied, turning and walking away. "They'll soon set you straight!"

CHAPTER ELEVEN

MORNING LIGHT SHONE THROUGH the six stained glass windows in the dining room, as June made her way from the foot of the staircase and stopped to see that Lucy was already hard at work.

"Breakfast's almost ready," Lucy explained, setting another plate on the table before turning to her. "I was just -"

Before she could finish, she knocked a glass, sending it rolling across the table. June hurried over and caught it just in time, taking care to set it back down in its proper place.

"Thank you so much," Lucy said. "I'm afraid that with my glasses broken, I've been a little more clumsy and fumble-prone than usual. And to be honest, I was already rather inclined in that regard. But you don't care about any of this. I still have some bread left, and it's not too bad, so I thought I'd bring some through for you."

"That's most kind," June told her, "but you mustn't feel as if you have to cater for me. I'm more than capable of making my own -"

"It's your first morning here," Lucy replied, interrupting her as she hurried to the door. "Well, your first morning for a good many years, at least. Oh, and how did you sleep?"

"How did I sleep?"

June immediately looked toward the sixth window, and for a moment she wasn't quite sure how to answer the question. After a few seconds she turned to see that Lucy had stopped in the doorway, and that she seemed rather keen to hear a response.

"Fine, I believe," June continued. "It's difficult to say. I was rather tired after my journey yesterday. In truth, I've been tired ever since I returned from the desert."

"You must tell me all about your adventures."

"Oh, I'd rather not get into detail," June protested, briefly thinking back to her time in the tunnels beneath the sand, and to the awful sight of Doctor Weaver being killed. She could only hope that Stella was coping with the loss. "It was rather... eventful."

"I'll bet," Lucy said with a smile. "Good gosh, I bet your feet have barely touched the ground since you returned, have they?"

"Something like that," June told her.

"I'll return shortly with something for you," Lucy replied, hurrying out of the room. "Just hold on and I shall find the softest part left on the loaf!"

"You really mustn't fuss," June said, before turning to the window as she heard a rustling sound outside. "I think..."

Her voice trailed off as the sound continued. Making her way over, June approached the sixth window and peered through the clearer pane of glass near the bottom. To her surprise, she saw a dark shape moving on the other side, and after a few more seconds she realized that she could see a large bear staring back at her. A moment later, as if to confirm that impression, she heard the bear's roar.

***

"I'm sorry to turn up like this," John said, still adjusting his collar as he stepped round from behind the corner. "You're quite a tricky person to track down."

"I had thought that the whole point of your... transformation was to blend in," June told him. "There aren't many bears roaming the English countryside."

"Now you're giving me notes?" he replied, raising an eyebrow.

"How did you find me?"

"I exhausted all other possibilities," he explained, "and then... I suppose deep down I always knew that the First Order would send you here eventually. They pick their operatives with great care, and they have a habit of sending them to confront events from their past. You were a schoolgirl here once, weren't you?"

"A long time ago."

"Little Sister June," he continued with a smile, "running around and having fun. I can hardly imagine such a thing."

"I'm not asking you to try to imagine it."

"I suppose that was before you were engaged in your current occupation," he added, looking her up and down. "The future was wide open and waiting for you. Do you ever wonder, June, what you might have become if you hadn't been kidnapped by the nuns of St. Jude's?"

"I wasn't kidnapped," she said firmly. "I was invited to join them, and I gratefully accepted."

"Whatever. The point is, you're back here now after so long away, and I just wanted to touch base and see how you're doing. How was Africa?"

"Eventful," she admitted. "I was sent -"

"I know the details," he replied, cutting her off. "I also know that after you left, the First Order sent a whole team to recover something from beneath the desert. It was a gate, I believe."

"The gate was destroyed."

"Nothing is ever truly destroyed," he countered. "At best, you just gave them a fun three-dimensional jigsaw puzzle, and I'm sure they're hard at work putting it back together. It'll take them time, but don't doubt for one second that they'll get there eventually. The question is, which gate did they acquire?"

"I believe it was..."

June's voice trailed off as she remembered the awful sights she'd seen down in the depths beneath the desert. No matter how many times she'd tried to convince herself that she must have been mistaken, she was unable to shake a sense of true dread, or to stop thinking of the painting that hung at St. Jude's; the idea that she'd seen even the slightest glimpse of Hell itself was almost impossible to believe, yet she also worried that she was in danger of rejecting reality.

"You don't have to say the words," John told her after a moment. "I'm fairly sure that I know the answer already."

"I saw the other side, briefly," she admitted. "I even met one of the... creatures from down there."

"That must have been a chastening experience," he replied. "For a nun, I mean."

"I should like to forget that it ever happened," she told him, "although I know I should not shy from the truth."

"June, there's something you need to understand," he said cautiously. "When the First Order is done with one of their operatives, they don't simply give them a fruit basket and thank them for all their work. They don't like leaving loose ends, if you catch my drift, and they're not shy when it comes to making people disappear. However, there's also a degree of cruelty to their methods, and they often like to try to break people in imaginative ways."

"I'm not sure that I follow."

"Have you ever heard of a place called Shadborne?"

"No. Should I have done?"

"It's a place where the First Order like to... terminate their employees. They need to get people ready for the place first, however, by cracking their minds. From what I can tell, I think they're keen to make sure that nothing has been kept from them, so they break their operatives so that they can more fully check for scraps. It's not a good place to end up, June. It's kind of the last stop on the First Order Express."

"I shall remember that warning if I'm ever asked to go there."

"The First Order don't ask," he said firmly. "You should know that by now." He checked his watch. "I should get going. I only returned recently from a little trip to Zurich, and I read something that I still need to digest properly. I'll pop by to see you again soon, though." Stepping back, he looked up at the windows of Holdham Hall. "Just remember what I said to you, June," he added. "Protect yourself. Guard yourself. Most of all, be on the lookout for anything they might use to try to get to you. Work out your greatest weakness, June, and try to neutralize it so they can't turn it against you." He looked past her, as if momentarily struck by something. "And be aware that it might come from the most unlikely of directions."

"Thank you for the warning," she replied, "but -"

"Sister June?" Lucy called out from somewhere in the distance. "Where are you?"

June turned to look; when she turned to John again, she saw no sign of him. She hurried to the corner and looked around the side of the building, but he seemed almost to have vanished into thin air. Although she wanted to call out to him, she realized with a heavy sigh that evidently he wasn't a man who liked to hang around and make small talk. He'd delivered his message, and now he was off again.

"Yoo hoo!" Lucy shouted from the front door. "Sister June, are you ready for breakfast? I have it all ready for you if you'd care to come to the table! Sister June, is everything alright?"

CHAPTER TWELVE

1945...

"SO THIS IS WHERE we leave our friend Napoleon Bonaparte," Mrs. Barker said at the head of the classroom, using a cane to tap the blackboard. "Think of that, girls. All the bluster, all the pomposity, and he ended up dying on a little island far from the empire he tried to create."

She looked around the room for a moment, clearly keen to make sure that the children were paying attention.

"But let his ignominious end not blind us," she continued, "to the greatness he possessed. There is a tendency in this country to belittle men of his sort, to make fun of them and pretend that their defeat was predestined all along. That was most certainly not the case with Mr. Bonaparte. I hope you understand, girls, that history could very easily have gone along a different course. How would you feel, for example, if we were all French?"

A murmur of disapproval spread across the room.

"You must think about how you just reacted," Mrs. Barker explained. "I won't have any of this anti-French nonsense, not in my classroom. And tomorrow we're going to move on to another period of that great country's history, one that I believe reflects upon our own story. This, after all, is the age of empires rising and falling, and while the two great wars are fresh in our minds we must not forget what came before. Indeed, we must not forget what led to those wars in the first place."

Although she found Mrs. Barker's lecture rather interesting, June couldn't help but turn her attention to Meredith, who was sitting at the next desk along. Ever since the class had started, June had noticed that her friend seemed particularly detached from the world, staring straight ahead with weary eyes; now, furrowing her brow, June realized that Meredith actually seemed to be falling asleep. Worried that this might attract Mrs. Barker's attention, June waited until their teacher had turned to the blackboard before reaching over with one leg to nudge Meredith and try to keep her awake.

"Are you okay?" she whispered.

Meredith nodded, but she was very clearly far from okay.

After glancing toward the front of the room to make sure that Mrs. Barker was still writing on the board, June turned to Meredith again.

"You're not okay," she said cautiously. "You look pale."

"When you go to sleep," Meredith replied, "do you wake up feeling better?"

"What do you mean?"

"Do you wake up feeling less tired? And with more energy?"

"I feel rested," June told her. "Sometimes I have bad dreams, but most of the time when I sleep I just... feel more energized when I wake up."

"For me, it's the opposite," Meredith whispered. "I feel more and more tired each morning. This morning I woke up and I felt so much worse than I did last night. I'm almost scared to go to bed again tonight, because I know I'll feel even worse tomorrow."

"You should tell Mrs. Barker."

Meredith shook her head.

"You really should," June continued. "There might be something wrong, something she knows how to fix. I know you're scared, Meredith, but I can come with you if it helps. You'd probably -"

"What is so interesting back there?" Mrs. Barker shouted, and June turned to see that she had finally turned around. "June and Meredith, evidently you're too busy to pay attention in my class. Go to my office immediately and wait for me there. Clearly, it's time for the pair of you to learn the meaning of the word discipline!"

***

Letting out a gasp, June dropped forward onto her knees. She winced, but she could already feel a bead of blood running down her bare back.

"There," Mrs. Barker said darkly, towering above her from behind. "I've been merciful this time. You only received ten lashes. The remaining twenty are suspended, but they will be added to the tally for your next infraction. Is that clear?"

"Yes," June stammered, barely able to get any words out at all.

"Now get up," Mrs. Barker snarled, before snapping her fingers at Meredith. "It's your turn."

"Wait," June said, turning and seeing that Meredith was even having trouble standing.

"Did you just tell me what to do?" Mrs. Barker asked.

"I'll take them," June said, looking up at her. "The lashes you're going to give to Meredith... I want them."

"Why would you ask such a thing?"

"I just think... it was my fault earlier," June

continued, "and Meredith's not very well. Please, Mrs. Barker, aren't I allowed to take the burden for her?" She waited for an answer. "I'm begging you."

"Do you hear that, Meredith?" Mrs. Barker asked, while keeping her eyes fixed very much on June's face. "Your new friend here wants to receive the punishment that's meant for you. What do we think about that, eh? Is she making a noble sacrifice that we should respect, or is she displaying an unprecedented lack of respect for the values I'm attempting to instill in all my pupils?" Again she paused, as if she was genuinely waiting for a response as she looked over at Meredith and then at June again. "How about both?"

"I'm just trying to help her," June stammered. "She's been through so much."

"You don't know what she's been through," Mrs. Barker sneered dismissively. "You seem to have a very high estimation of your own opinion, young lady, but I'm going to knock that out of you. Meredith, you may leave us, but I want you to go to the kitchen and clean every surface until it shines brighter than the sun. If I find even the tiniest spot of dirt later, I will make you weep like you've never wept before. Is that understood?"

"I don't want June to get hurt," Meredith said, stepping forward. "Please, can I just take my punishment?"

"I've made my decision," Mrs. Barker told

her. "June will take your ten lashes."

"But -"

"Make that fifteen."

"Mrs. Barker, I -"

"Twenty, Meredith."

"Please -"

"Twenty-five."

"But I only -"

"Thirty!"

Meredith opened her mouth to reply, but she just about managed to hold back. With tears in her eyes, she turned and looked down at June, and then she hurried out of the room while muttering something to herself. As the door swung shut, June listened to the sound of Meredith's footsteps running away along the corridor, and then she tensed every muscle in her body as she heard the distinctive sound of Mrs. Barker stepping up behind her.

"When will my work ever be done?" the headmistress asked wearily. "When will I ever run out of children to discipline? I have been working so hard for so long, but none of you ever truly learn, do you? Even if you do, another miscreant will be along shortly. Sometimes I think that I must be at my post forever, always waiting for the endless supply of girls to come to an end, never quite gaining the rest I so richly deserve. And what will be left for me? What possible happiness can I gain?"

"Are you going to hurt me?" June whispered.

"Hurt you?" Mrs. Barker replied. "Child, hurting you would do no good, not in the long run. I could hurt you without even breaking a sweat. Instead, I am going to bring you to a place of understanding. I am going to make you see the world through my eyes, so that you bow down before me and promise that you'll never doubt me again. I am going to make sure that ultimately you know I'm right, and that you praise me for my actions."

"Never," June replied.

"What was that?"

"I said I'll never see the world how you see it," June continued, even though she knew she was only going to get herself into more and more trouble. "I'll always know that you're wrong, and that -"

Suddenly the whip cracked and June screamed. Feeling a bursting pain running diagonally up her back, she slumped forward again, barely managing to hold herself up. The pain was so much worse than before, so much more intense, and for a few seconds June felt as if she might be about to pass out. She clenched her teeth, determined to show as little weakness as possible, refusing to surrender the last traces of her dignity. A moment later Mrs. Barker whipped her again, and this time June barely managed to stay on her hands and knees. Finally, as tears began to run down her face, she looked at the door and saw a hint of movement, and she realized that Meredith had returned to watch her awful punishment.

In that instant Mrs. Barker struck her again with the whip, then again, until finally the fifth blow brought so much pain that June screamed and slumped down unconscious against the floor.

CHAPTER THIRTEEN

1982...

"SO WHAT'S THE PLAN for today?" Lucy asked as she took a seat at the other end of the dining room's long table. "I must admit, it's so nice to have someone here at last. I've been getting rather bored, pottering around on my own."

"I think I might take another look at Mrs. Barker's records," June explained. "I might be wrong, of course, but I rather suspect that the daylight hours are unlikely to reveal much about any ghostly inhabitants of the house."

"Right!" Lucy exclaimed. "I hadn't thought about that, but I suppose ghosts are much more likely to come out at night, aren't they? Why do you think that is, anyway? Are they just creatures of the shadows, determined to stay hidden? Or could there be some other reason?"

"I'm really not sure," June told her. "Perhaps -"

"I love a good ghost story," Lucy continued. "They're just so spooky, aren't they? Oh, I know I probably shouldn't be so into them. After all, they don't really fit with the whole..." She leaned forward and lowered her voice a little. "God thing," she added, "but there's just something about them that's just so utterly compelling."

"God thing?" June said, raising an eyebrow. "I must admit, I've never heard our religious calling described in such a way."

"Of course not," Lucy replied, forcing a big smile. "Sorry, I suppose that just slipped out."

"What convent did you say you were from again?"

"St. Wendy's," Lucy reminded her. "You probably haven't heard of it. Nobody ever has."

"I didn't know that there *was* a Saint Wendy."

"Well, it's Gwendoline, really," Lucy continued, and now she seemed increasingly uncomfortable. "Saint Gwendoline."

"Indeed," June said cautiously. "Well, I'm sure that we can keep ourselves busy for the duration of the day. As well as inspecting the records, I would like to come up with some kind of plan of action for tonight. In the absence of any firm instructions from the First Order, I can only assume that we are to determine the true nature of any presence that might be here and -"

"And find out the truth about the place?" Lucy suggested.

"That would be rather good," June told her, although once again she couldn't shake the feeling that something was a little 'off' about Sister Lucy, as if she barely seemed like a nun at all. "I must say, by the time night falls I would like to have a better idea of what's going on here."

"I'm sure we will," Lucy replied. "And I, of course, am at your disposal. I defer to your judgment in every matter regarding this situation, and I hope you will use me as you see fit."

"I shall certainly be glad of your help," June said, preferring to treat her associate as an equal rather than as a subordinate. "And now, if you don't mind, I would very much like to finish this bread so that I can get to work."

***

A few hours later, sitting in Mrs. Barker's office, June continued to pore over the various records she'd carried through from the next room. No matter how hard she focused on the documents, she found one curious factor that made no sense at all; as she heard Lucy making her way into the office, she leaned back in Mrs. Barker's chair and felt as if she might be on the verge of giving up.

"Nothing," she said, unable to hide a sense of frustration.

"I beg your pardon?" Lucy replied.

"These files are so detailed," June explained, holding up a couple of the folders, "but they only run up to the end of 1944, which was shortly before I arrived. In fact, Meredith is one of the last children included, but the section concerning her death is missing. It's almost as if somebody came along and took certain documents while leaving others."

"Why would they do that?" Lucy asked.

"Your guess is as good as mine," June told her, setting the folders down and taking a look at several others. "I don't see any other explanation, though. Someone as fastidious and detail-orientated as Elspeth Barker certainly wouldn't have simply given up keeping records at some point."

"Were you hoping to find something about your own time here at the school?"

"I confess to feeling a stir of curiosity," June told her, "although I don't want you to think that I'm being self-centered. I just find myself wondering whether my own time here is the key to the mystery in some way. And then there's the whole problem of room thirty, and the fact that so many of the children in that room died. I feel as if I'm going round and round in circles, constantly getting closer to an explanation but missing the bigger picture because..."

She hesitated, trying to make sense of her frustration.

"Because I'm not seeing the wood for the trees," she added finally. "I can't shake the fear that I'm missing something big, one major fact that would allow all the other pieces to slot into place." She began to open the various drawers in the desk, more out of desperation than hope. "All I find so far is -"

Stopping suddenly, she saw something very familiar in the bottom drawer. A shiver of dread passed through her chest as she reached down and picked up the same whip that many years earlier had cut into her own back. As she turned the whip around, she even saw that the cord was slightly stained, and she wondered whether this might have been her own blood. No matter how hard she tried to ignore this memory, to pretend that she had moved past it all, she knew deep down that each of those thrashings remained deeply ingrained in her mind; she also thought back to her darkest moments at Switzerland's Castle Vertigon, and she finally joined the dots between the whippings she'd received at Holdham Hall and her willingness to punish herself the same way in the castle's cold stone rooms.

"We are all," she whispered now, "a product of our upbringing."

"What was that?" Lucy asked merrily.

"Nothing," June said, setting the whip back into the drawer. "Just a little reminder of a day many years ago. Two days, in fact."

"So do you think there might be another set of records?" Lucy continued. "Did someone perhaps come and separate them?"

"It's possible," June said, preferring to focus on the mystery at hand, "but somehow my instincts are telling me that these records are entirely intact. Nobody has been rooting around in them. It's almost as if..."

She thought for a moment, trying to make sense of the conflicting ideas rushing through her mind.

"It's almost as if Mrs. Barker kept fastidious records for a number of years," she continued, "and then, shortly before I arrived, she just... stopped."

Picking up another folder, she opened it and found various documents and receipts for work that had been done around Holdham Hall. She leafed through these receipts and saw one from 1940 for some new fencing in the garden, another from 1942 for some medication, and another from 1943 for the repair of a window in the dining room; she paused for a few seconds, thinking back to the single clear panel in the sixth window, and she realized that this panel must have been replaced at some point, perhaps after being accidentally broken. Certainly this panel was the odd one out, and it also happened to be the panel through which the ghost supposedly stared.

"If you look into that part of the window," she remembered one of the girls telling her many years earlier, "and see a ghost, you won't be long for this world."

"And anyone who looks into that part of the window," another girl had insisted, "sees a ghost eventually."

"Perhaps she just got bored," Lucy suggested.

June looked up at her.

"Of the paperwork, I mean," Lucy continued. "Old Mrs. Barker... that was her name, wasn't it? Anyway, people tire of things eventually, so isn't it possible that she just got a little older and decided to not do it anymore? People *do* change over time. Nobody's one person forever."

"No," June replied, pausing for a moment longer before getting to her feet, "you're right, they aren't. And that's especially true of Mrs. Barker, because she most certainly changed, even in the short time that I knew her. When I first arrived here she was a terrible firebrand, and so very strict. Something altered in her, however, and later she became much calmer. Almost benevolent. I never really stopped to wonder why that might have been."

"Any ideas?" Lucy asked.

"It was after she punished me," June continued, thinking back to that awful day. "Of course, first I showed a little weakness, despite my best efforts. And I met somebody who might hold the key to all of this."

CHAPTER FOURTEEN

1945...

OPENING HER EYES, JUNE saw bright light shining through a narrow, rather thin window. She blinked a few times, and then – hearing a rustling sound – she turned to see a young woman sitting at a desk in the corner of the room.

"Ah," the woman said with a smile, getting to her feet and wandering over, "you're awake. That's good." She pulled a thermometer from her pocket and held it out. "Mouth open, please."

June obediently opened her mouth, and then she waited as the woman slid the thermometer in and checked the reading.

"Okay, that's good," she muttered, making her way back to the desk and noting the result on a piece of paper. "There's no sign of... Well, you're the very picture of health, apart from those horrible cuts on your back. Those will heal, but I'm afraid you might end up with a few scars. Or you might not. I've tried my best to apply a little balm and sometimes that does absolute wonders. The only thing to do now, really, is to wait and see and to hope for the best. And, perhaps, a few little prayers here and there wouldn't go amiss."

Sitting up, June found that she was in an unfamiliar part of the house. She was sitting on a bed, and as she looked around the room she saw that it had all the trappings of a small doctor's surgery. Turning to the woman again, she saw that she was wearing the dress of a nun, and something about her immediately struck her as kind and comforting. At the same time, feeling a sore pain on her back, she pulled a little further along the bed.

"My name is Martha," the woman explained. "Sister Martha, really, but you can call me Martha. I'm the nurse here at Holdham Hall."

"Nurse?"

"I was just like you once," Martha continued. "I was a pupil here, and I was chosen to go to the convent. But I missed the place, and I missed Mrs. Barker, and I begged the sisters to let me return. Eventually they acquiesced and here I am, helping to patch up the girls and deal with any... maladies that they might develop. Obviously I'm not a doctor, but with the war going on we all have to roll up our sleeves and do our best."

"The war's over," June replied.

"So it is," Martha said, turning to her with a smile, "but the mindset continues, does it not? I think you should know that Mrs. Barker feels absolutely terrible for what happened. She's been under a lot of stress lately. That's not an excuse, but she called me to her office to fetch you and... I've not seen her in such a state for quite a long time. You must understand that for all her bluster, Elspeth... I mean, Mrs. Barker... is just a woman like any other, with all the attendant qualities and flaws. Right now, in fact, she's deep in prayer, trying to find some way to atone for her sins."

"She is?" June said, puzzled by this news and not quite believing that it could possibly be true.

"I've been here for a while now," Martha explained, sitting on the edge of the desk. "Every time I think I've seen it all, that Holdham Hall has thrown everything it can at me, I'm surprised again by some new development. I'm sorry, we didn't meet until now, but that's because I prefer to stay in the background. People only really see me if they're sick, or if they've sprained an ankle or suffered some other mishap. That's just the way I like things to be. I suppose you could say that I'm a solitary soul at heart."

"Where's Meredith?" June asked cautiously.

"Meredith?" Martha paused for a moment. "Ah, yes," she continued, "I know Meredith. Lovely child, very sweet, a little meek and could do with some more oomph but otherwise she's no trouble at all. Yes, I rather like her."

"Is she alright?"

"As far as I know," Martha replied, "she's as alright as the rest of us here. But if you think I should check on her, I'd be happy to make a note and pull her in for a chat."

"I'm not sure," June said, wincing as she felt the painful cuts on her back shifting beneath the bandages. "I'm not sure that anyone's alright here. I haven't been at Holdham Hall for very long, but I'm really not sure that I like it very much."

"That's to be expected," Martha told her.

"Can I go?" June asked, looking at the door.

"I want to see you again every day around this time," Martha replied, "just so that I can check those bandages. Do we have an understanding?"

Nodding, June hurried toward the door, but she stopped as Martha reached out and put a hand on her shoulder. The woman's touch was cold, and June had to really fight to resist the urge to pull away.

"Remarkable," Martha mused after a few seconds. "Truly remarkable. I must say, June, it's good to have you here but also a little on the puzzling side." She paused again, still touching June's shoulder as if she couldn't quite believe what she was feeling, until finally she pulled her hand away. "Go," she added finally, with a hint of sadness in her voice. "Play with the other girls. I think it might be good for you."

***

Making her way along the corridor that led to her room, June felt as if her legs might buckle at any moment. She couldn't shake a strange sense of unease, as if she truly didn't belong at Holdham Hall, but she told herself that everything would be alright just as soon as she could get some sleep. And then, as she reached the door to room thirty, she found her way blocked by Meredith.

"What did you do?" Meredith sneered.

"Are you alright?" June asked, trying to smile. "Meredith, I -"

"What did you do?" Meredith shouted angrily, shaking with rage. "Why did you bleed?"

"What are you talking about?"

"Why did you bleed all over Mrs. Barker's nice floor?" Meredith continued, clearly on the verge of losing control. "I thought you were my friend, June! Why would you do something like that?"

"I thought I was helping," June stammered,

shocked by her reception. "Can we talk about this later? I -"

"You're not helping!" Meredith snarled. "How can you possibly ever have thought that? You're making everything a million times worse!"

"But -"

"It was okay here before you arrived," Meredith continued, with tears streaming down her face now. "Do you understand that? I was scared and tired, but at least I knew exactly what was happening. Then you turned up out of the blue, and you've made everything so confusing!" She took a step back, bumping against the side of the door, and for a moment she seemed to be on the verge of losing control. "I thought you were going to be my friend," she whimpered. "I thought I finally had a new friend and I thought you were going to make everything better. I thought we were going to be friends forever!"

"Meredith, I -"

"But I hate you!" Meredith shouted, turning and running away along the corridor. "I hate you so much! I never want to see your face ever again!"

"Meredith, wait!" June called out, before sighing as she realized that she was too late. Meredith had already run round the corner, and her footsteps rang out until eventually they faded into the distance, leaving June standing all alone. "I don't understand," she continued. "What did I do wrong?"

Looking around, she realized that there was no sign of anyone else. Supposing that the other girls were in another of Mrs. Barker's classes, she stepped into room thirty and saw her suitcase under the bed, and in that moment she realized that there was one obvious solution to her problem. She'd always prided herself on being obedient and well-behaved, but something was very wrong at Holdham Hall and she was starting to feel as if her very presence at the school was some kind of terrible mistake. She thought back to everything Mr. Holden had told her when he'd dropped her off, to all the promises and reassurances he'd made, but his words sounded so hollow now and she was already starting to come up with a better plan.

"Fine," she said, clenching her fists, "if no-one wants me here, then I won't be here. You can keep your rotten, stinking school. As soon as it gets dark and no-one'll be able to see me, I'm getting out of this place and none of you will ever have to see me ever again!"

CHAPTER FIFTEEN

1982...

"IT'S A JOLLY COLD day, isn't it?" Lucy said, trudging across the lawn just a few paces behind June. "Then again, I suspected we were in for a cold spell in the new year. I don't want to toot my own horn, but sometimes I feel that I'm rather good at guessing what the weather's going to be."

"That's wonderful," June replied, barely paying any attention whatsoever as she marched toward the treeline ahead.

"I know this might sound like a terrible thing to say," Lucy continued, "but I shall be glad when I'm back at the convent. St. Wendy's might not be everyone's cup of tea, but it's home for me, and it's where I feel most comfortable. I've always been that way inclined and -"

"St. Wendy's?" June asked, stopping and turning to her. "Or St. Gwendoline's?"

"Uh... both, really," Lucy replied, stopping just in time to avoid clattering straight into June. "I suppose technically it's called St. Gwendoline's, you're right about that, but a group of us there call it St. Wendy's because... I think we're just being silly."

"And who *was* St. Gwendoline?" June asked. "I'm sorry, I'm a little fuzzy on that. Sister Margaret always used to tell me that it was the one blind spot I had in my studies, and I worked so hard to drum them all into my head but I never quite succeeded."

"Who was she?" Lucy said, before pausing for a moment. "She was supposedly born in the fifth century. She was Britannic, I believe, and according to some of the more unusual legends she had three..." Her voice trailed off, and after a moment – clearly feeling increasingly uncomfortable – she tapped her own chest. "You know. Of these."

"Three breasts?"

Lucy nodded.

"I remember now," June continued. "She's known as St. Gwenn in the records I've read."

"That's right," Lucy said, forcing a smile. "According to legend, she was kidnapped at least twice by Anglo-Saxon pirates, and she had to make her own way home to her father's castle. Eventually she settled in Dorset, and some raiders turned up one day and... well, she died a rather horrible death."

"Yes, she did," June said, watching Lucy carefully and trying to understand her body language. "There's a shrine, is there not? Some say that the site of her burial is a location where many miracles have occurred."

"Absolutely," Lucy replied. "Our convent is nowhere near that, it's up north, but we still feel a very close tie to her story."

"And she famously battled some kind of wild beast," June added. "A serpent, wasn't it?"

"Possibly," Lucy said. "I'm not sure, I don't remember all the details. Yes, I think I *do* remember something about her fighting a serpent. Or was it a dragon?"

"I'm not sure," June told her, having made up the part about the serpent in an attempt to test her companion's claims. More certain than ever that something wasn't quite right with her, June tried to work out whether to confront her with the truth or to wait and see what she did next. "I need to find something in the forest," she added finally. "Are you sure you're up for a little walk? If you'd rather wait at the school, that would be fine by me and certainly a lot more comfortable for you."

"Oh, no, I'd love to come with you," Lucy replied. "Please, won't you lead the way?"

***

"It's really rather dense out here, isn't it?" Lucy continued a short while later, struggling to pick her way past curling bramble loops that rose up from the undergrowth. "I'm sorry, I might have missed the explanation, but can you remind me again... what are we doing out here, exactly?"

"Searching for something," June replied.

"What kind of -"

"It's just a crazy thought," June continued. "There was a nurse here at the school years ago, her name was Martha. I barely met her at all, but I think she might be the key to everything."

"Right," Lucy said, ducking under a low branch and almost getting stuck on more brambles. She had to take a few seconds to pull her habit clear. "And she's... out here, is she?"

"I wouldn't have thought so," June replied. "At least, not in the way that you mean."

Stopping, she looked around for a moment as if she felt utterly lost.

"It's so different in the daylight," she added with more than a hint of frustration. "The last time I came this way was thirty-seven years ago, in the middle of the night."

"What were you doing out here in the middle of the night?" Lucy asked.

"Running away."

"Running away? From where?" Lucy waited for an answer. "You don't mean from the school, do you? Why would you ever have been running away from the school? I rather got the impression that you loved your time there."

June turned to her.

"*That's* the impression you got from everything I've been telling you?"

"Well, no school is perfect," Lucy pointed out, as if she'd somehow missed almost the entire point of the situation. "Still, Holdham Hall is out in the countryside, which is a kind of paradise, and you were surrounded by other girls your own age. As someone who attended a school in the city, let me tell you that a place like this would have felt like the most wonderful school in the entire world. I just can't imagine why anyone would ever want to run away."

"I had my reasons," June told her. "The truth is, I was just a child. A precocious child, and a child who acted well beyond her years. I might not have entirely understood what was going on, but I'm starting to think that my gut instincts at the time were trying to tell me something."

"About the school?"

"About all of it," June said, looking back the way they'd just come. Beyond the trees, she could see a few patches of light and the distant dark shape of Holdham Hall silhouetted against the gray midday sky. "I've been in some unusual situations over the years," she added, "but never one that quite felt like such a puzzle. It's almost as if this place has been waiting more than three decades for me to come back and shine a light on what was really happening. Almost as if I never quite finished what I was doing here in the first place."

She watched the trees for a moment longer before turning to see a somewhat bemused expression on Lucy's face.

"Right," Lucy said after a moment. "I see."

"Do you?"

"Not really. I'm afraid I still don't understand."

"Something was happening here," June told her, "something that my ten-year-old mind was just too young and possibly too naive to understand. For all that I seemed very grown-up at the time, I was still just a little girl. I think I missed something rather huge, but that's not the mystery. The mystery is why, all this time later, the First Order has sent me back here to resolve it all. What is it that they want me to see?"

"No idea," Lucy replied, before nodding at something in the distance. "It couldn't have anything to do with those stones, could it?"

June turned and looked at the long grass. For a few seconds she couldn't work out what Lucy meant, but finally she spotted the tops of a few curved stones poking out from the shadowed end of an almost-clearing; stepping forward, she felt a flicker of dread in her chest as she realized that they'd finally found what she was looking for. She hesitated, worried about what she was going to learn, and then she waded through the grass before stopping again as she reached the first of the stones.

"What are they?" Lucy asked, sounding a little breathless now as she struggled to keep up. "Sister June? Was I right? Are these what you were looking for?"

"They certainly are," June said, before grabbing clumps of the long grass and ripping it out of the ground so that she could see the first stone better. "There has to be a reason for them being here, and when I was young I didn't realize that I should look more closely. I suppose I was too busy being scared."

"But what are they?" Lucy said again, stopping behind her. Squinting slightly, she took a pair of glasses from her pocket and slipped them on, and then she leaned closer. "I can't quite read the words on there," she continued, "but they look almost like... gravestones."

"They are," June whispered, looking past this stone and seeing dozens more nearby. "And there are an awful lot of them, don't you think?"

CHAPTER SIXTEEN

1945...

HOLDHAM HALL STOOD IN darkness, with only a few lights at a handful of windows, as an owl hooted in the distance. A few seconds later, once she was sure that the coast was clear and that she wouldn't be spotted, June ducked out from the shadows and began to carry her suitcase across the lawn.

Glancing over her shoulder every few seconds, she told herself that as soon as she reached the treeline she'd be fine. After that she'd have to make her way to the same road where Mr. Holden had dropped her off a few days earlier, and then she was going to have to work out where to go next. In truth, her plan so far hadn't extended any further than escaping from the grounds of the school, but she supposed that somehow everything was going to be alright eventually. She'd already been praying all afternoon, asking for guidance and help, and she told herself that anything was better than staying at Holdham Hall and enduring even another minute of the school's terrible atmosphere.

Reaching the trees, she dropped down onto her knees and looked back across the lawn. A few lights were flickering in the dining room, and in some of the upstairs rooms, but overall the school looked almost desolate. She thought of Meredith somewhere in there, no doubt still full of anger, and she briefly felt bad for leaving without saying goodbye. At the same time, she thought back to Meredith's rage and fury earlier, and she quickly reminded herself that running away was the best option.

"Goodbye, everyone," she whispered. "I wish nothing but the best for all of you."

Getting to her feet, she began to push her way through the forest, struggling to avoid the brambles as she tried to work out the best route to the road.

***

"Ow!" she hissed, as yet another bramble caught on her leg, scratching the skin despite her best efforts to pull away. "Can you – ow!"

Stopping for a moment, June felt as if she'd made a terrible mistake. Sure, walking through the forest minimized the risk that she might be spotted, but she had gravely underestimated the discomfort that would be caused by so many brambles and thorns. She felt sure that her legs must be cut to ribbons by now, almost matching her bloodied back, but she knew that she'd already gone too far to turn around now. In the darkness, barely able to see anything except a few patches of moonlight here and there, she reminded herself that hopefully this was the worst part of the journey.

Somewhere far off, an owl hooted again.

"It's alright for you," June muttered. "You can fly. Some of us are stuck down here, making our way through the thickets."

The owl hooted yet again, almost as if offering a reply.

Telling herself that there was no point dawdling, June began to set off again. After just a couple more steps, however, she bumped against something very solid; looking down, she was just about able to see – in the faint glow of moonlight – a pale stone with a rounded top section. She reached out and touched the stone, finding that it was unsurprisingly very cold, and then she crouched down to take a better look at the letters carved into the front.

"Jan... Janice?" she whispered, before spotting some numbers further down. "Janice something?"

Pulling back, she realized that she'd found a gravestone. At that moment the clouds shifted enough to let some more moonlight through, and to her horror June saw several more stones, all of the exact same design and placed in a series of neat rows. The sight was so surreal that for a few seconds she couldn't quite believe that it was real, and she wondered whether she might be imagining things. Finally she crawled over to another of the stones and saw the name Emily, followed by a third stone bearing the name Victoria.

Getting to her feet, she looked around the clearing and counted many more stones, and a shiver ran through her bones as she began to wonder how and why so many people could have ended up being buried in this small patch of land so close to the school.

"How many people have died here?" she asked out loud, as she carried her suitcase between the stones, looking down at each of them in turn.

She knew that a number of girls had perished during their time at the school, and that they seemed to be mostly connected to room thirty. She'd never realized that just so many had died, however, and she couldn't help but feel that something must be terribly wrong. Although she knew that Mrs. Barker certainly seemed to be a tyrant, she couldn't quite bring herself to believe that the headmistress had been whipping so many girls to death, and she also knew that such terrible behavior would certainly have been uncovered by the authorities. Reaching the farthest row of stones, she turned to look back the way she'd just come, and once again she tried to count the graves, only to give up as she realized that the precise number was perhaps unimportant.

Reaching up, June made the sign of the cross against her chest, before closing her eyes and offering a brief prayer for the souls of so many who had died. She continued to whisper to herself for a few more seconds, and then – when she opened her eyes again – she let out a gasp as she saw that there were now lots of young girls standing in the darkness, each one next to one of the gravestones.

"Who are you?" June asked, taking a step back, dropping her suitcase in the process. "I didn't mean to disturb you, I only -"

"You shouldn't be here," one of the girls snarled, stepping forward into the moonlight, revealing an angry face with features that appeared to have sunk into the recesses of her skull. "You're not welcome here with us."

"I'm sorry," June stammered, trying not to panic. "I didn't even know that there was anyone here. I was just -"

"Leave!" another of the girls hissed, her voice filled with venom. "Before it's too late!"

"I'm leaving," June said, reaching for her suitcase before stumbling and turning, opting to run instead. "I'm sorry!" she called out again. "Forgive me, I didn't mean to disturb you!"

Catching her foot on the edge of yet another gravestone, June fell down hard against the ground. She turned and saw the dead girls still standing by their graves, and a moment later the ghostly figures began to step forward.

"No!" June yelled, scrambling to her feet again and racing through the undergrowth, desperate to get away at all costs. "Leave me alone!"

No matter how hard she tried to convince herself that the ghostly girls couldn't possibly be real, June was unable to stop running as she tried to get as far from the graves as possible. She almost tripped and stumbled several more times, and she almost slammed into a number of trees, but she managed to keep running until finally – with no warning – she emerged at the edge of the forest and stopped just in time to see the road snaking past. Spinning around, she looked back into the forest, but clouds had drifted back in front of the moon and she could no longer see any figures in the darkness. The dead girls could easily have been just a few feet away, or they could have never been there at all.

Hearing a motor in the distance, June turned just in time to see a truck's headlights approaching around a bend in the road. The vehicle began to slow, coming to a halt nearby, and June saw a man staring out at her from the driver's seat.

"Hey!" the man shouted, waving at her. "Who are you? What are you doing out here so late at night?"

Frozen in place, June opened her mouth to reply but at the last second she held back. Part of her wanted to be picked up and taken away, but all manner of fears had begun to fill her mind.

"I see you there!" the man yelled, still waving. "Young girl, what are you doing here? Are you all by yourself? Come over here and I can take you to the town! Come on, there's no need to be scared!"

Terrified that he might return her to the school, June turned and ran again, ducking back into the forest even as the man continued to call out to her. Telling herself that she had to avoid everyone, including the strange girls, she raced through the darkness in a desperate attempt to find a place where she could hide and perhaps come up with a better plan.

CHAPTER SEVENTEEN

1982...

"MY WORD," JUNE SAID, lifting up the battered, moldy old suitcase from the mud, "it's still here after so many years."

"What is?" Lucy asked.

For a moment, June could only turn the suitcase around as she remembered how important it had once seemed. Following her parents' deaths, she'd had to pack all her remaining possessions into one small case; anything that didn't fit had been left behind. She'd been clutching the case on her journey to Holdham Hall with that kind Mr. Holden, and she still recalled how the handle had felt in her hand when he'd dropped her at the entrance gate.

"I'm terribly sorry I can't drive you to the

door," he'd told her, "but I'm awfully late for an appointment. You don't mind following that path to the schoolhouse, do you? The office sent a letter on ahead, telling them to expect you."

"Of course," June had replied, although deep down she'd been absolutely terrified. "Thank you for everything, Mr. Holden. You and the others have been so kind."

He'd driven away, leaving June standing all alone clutching the suitcase. Now, as she wiped some dirt from the case, June marveled at the fact that it had remained hidden in the undergrowth for so many years. She'd dropped it on that awful night when she'd run from the supposed ghosts, and she'd never had a chance to go back for it. Setting it on the ground, she knelt in the mud and carefully opened the case, revealing the clothes and hairbrush she'd packed on the night she'd planned to run away from Holdham Hall forever.

"The plans of children," she whispered.

"What is it?" Lucy asked, picking her way over. "It looks like a suitcase."

"That's because it is," June said, before gently closing the case.

"Was it just there in the mud?"

"It's of no importance."

"But -"

"It's really not important," June said again, getting to her feet while holding the suitcase, then turning to look at all the gravestones. For a moment, she wondered whether the ghostly little girls might appear again. "One mustn't allow oneself to become too wrapped up in the past. At least, not in the parts of the past that no longer matter."

"I'm afraid this all seems very cryptic to me," Lucy told her. "Or, I suppose, it could be that I'm rather slow on the uptake."

"I'm sorry," June replied, "but I'm still trying to work it all out myself." She turned to Lucy. "Once I have a better idea, I shall be sure to -"

Stopping suddenly, she saw sunlight glinting in the lenses of Lucy's glasses.

"Is everything alright?" Lucy asked after a moment.

"I thought... I'm sorry, but I thought you broke your only pair."

"My only pair of what?"

"Of glasses," June reminded her, as once again her suspicions were stirred and she found herself questioning the other woman's claims. "When I first arrived, you broke them and you said you had no spare pair with you. You told me that you were going to be positively blind as a bat for the rest of our time here."

"Oh, yes," Lucy said nervously, "I *did* say that, didn't I?" She reached up and touched her glasses, adjusting their position. "I found another pair," she added for a few seconds. "Silly old me, it turns out that I'd packed my spare pair after all. I found them last night in my bag, and let me tell you, it was quite a relief to see them again. Now I shall hopefully be of much more use to you going forward. If you want me to help, that is."

"Indeed," June replied, not quite sure that she believed that rather unlikely story. "Might I ask you a favor?"

"Anything."

"Would you mind checking each of these stones," she continued, "and jotting down as much as you can read? I know that most of the stones are illegible now, but you might be able to make out some dates and scraps of names."

"What do you want those for?" Lucy asked.

"I suppose I'm just trying to be thorough," June explained. "In the meantime, I must return to the main building. I have a hunch that there's something rather important that I've been missing in the dining room. In fact, I feel sure that there must be something interesting in that sixth window."

***

As she reached the lawn in front of Holdham Hall, still carrying the little suitcase she'd brought to the place more than three decades earlier, June was still lost in thought. She glanced toward the windows that overlooked the dining room, and then she stopped for a moment and looked all around.

For a few seconds she imagined all the girls playing on the grass. She remembered her own days at the school, and she spotted the bench where she'd sat during her lunch breaks. Although she hadn't been at Holdham Hall for very long, and she hadn't made many friends during that time, she was still struck by a melancholy sense of nostalgia for the fifty or so girls she'd met, and she found herself wondering where they all were now; some of them, she supposed, would have families of their own, while others might have gone into different areas of employment and some might even have died. She thought of all the lives, all the potential, and she hoped that they were all happy.

Glancing at the windows again, she told herself that -

Suddenly she froze as she saw a face at the sixth window. She told herself that she had to be wrong, but a set of blurred features were just about visible through the glass; a fraction of a second later the face vanished, just before June had a change to call out.

"Anyone who sees a ghost at the sixth window will die," she remembered one of the girls telling her, many years ago. "There's no coming back from that."

A shiver ran through her bones, but she quickly reminded herself that there was no point submitting to childish superstitions. She began to make her way across the lawn, determined to get to the truth; once she was inside the building, she set the suitcase down and then walked to the door that led into the dining room, and she stopped as she saw that there was absolutely no sign of anyone. She wasn't quite sure what she'd expected, but there was certainly no ghostly figure watching from the shadows. Looking over at the sixth window, however, June thought back to the face she'd spotted just a moment earlier; far from seeming less real now, that face was actually becoming clearer in her mind.

"Who are you?" she whispered, stepping into the room and making her way past the dining room table, approaching the window. "What do you want?"

Reaching the window, she peered at the clearer pane of glass in the bottom corner. This was the exact spot, she realized, where the ghostly figure must have been standing. The glass was mottled and warped, providing little in the way of a view, and June wondered whether anyone in this particular position could even have seen her out on the lawn. Indeed, as she continued to squint and peer at the glass, she realized that the only thing she could see was the faintest hint of her own reflection.

"So much for a ghost," she muttered, "or -"

Hearing footsteps, she turned and looked

across the dining room; the sound ended abruptly, but June couldn't shake the feeling that she had company.

"Lucy?" she called out. "Is that you?"

She waited.

Silence.

"Lucy, are you back already?" she continued. "That seems rather quick. Did you get all the names from those gravestones?"

Again, she heard nothing but silence. She swallowed hard, and then – supposing that perhaps the sound had been caused by something else – she turned to look at the window again. She saw the crack running up the wall and thought of its connection to the bed high up in room thirty, and she felt once more as if she had to be missing something important. So many girls had apparently seen a ghost while looking through the window, and according to childish gossip they'd all died; assuming for a moment that these claims were true, June wondered exactly how all these disparate elements could possibly be linked.

Hearing the footsteps again, she turned to look back at the door.

"Lucy, if -"

In that moment she froze, as she saw a familiar figure standing out in the hallway, staring back at her with cold dead eyes.

"What are you doing here?" June

stammered, unable to look away. "Meredith, it's me! It's June! I came back!"

CHAPTER EIGHTEEN

1945...

SLOWLY OPENING HER EYES, June saw a silhouetted figure standing over her, almost blocking the sun. She blinked and held up a hand, and now the figure was gone, but a moment later she heard a rustling sound in the undergrowth.

"June?" Meredith said. "What are you doing here?"

Sitting up, June turned and saw Meredith standing nearby. Looking past her, June saw the lawn and Holdham Hall, and she realized that during the night she'd wandered and wandered until finally passing out. She remembered running from the ghostly girls by the graves, and when she looked down she realized that she must have dropped her suitcase somewhere along the way. For a few seconds, unable to quite pull her thoughts together properly, she felt somewhat dazed.

"Did you run away?" Meredith asked. "I'm sorry I was harsh to you, June, but..."

She looked over her shoulder for a moment, watching the other girls playing on the lawn, and then she turned to June again.

"I don't know why you came here," she continued. "The other girls and I... I mean, we..."

Her voice trailed off again.

"I'm sorry," June said, hauling herself up, feeling various twinges and aches as she began to brush herself down. "I didn't mean to cause trouble."

"You're lucky that Mrs. Barker didn't come and do the register with us this morning," Meredith explained, "or she would've realized that you were missing, and then you'd have been in so much trouble."

"She didn't do the register? Why not?"

"I don't know," Meredith replied, "but the nurse did it instead. I suppose she noticed you weren't there, but she didn't get angry. She's a little bit nicer than Mrs. Barker."

"Evidently," June murmured, before pausing for a moment. She still wanted to get away from Holdham Hall, but at the same time she felt now that simply running off might be a bad idea. "I think

I should find a change of clothes," she continued finally, before hearing her own belly rumble. "And I'm hungry. I'm so very hungry. I haven't eaten since I got here."

"You haven't?"

"No," she said, turning to Meredith. "I missed dinner, and then I was poorly at lunch, and there hasn't been any breakfast and -"

Before she could finish, her belly rumbled again.

"I'm starving," she added.

"We should find you some food, then," Meredith suggested. "I'm sorry again, June. I was so horrible to you, but it was only because I was in shock. When I saw Mrs. Barker hurting you, and I saw the blood... I'm sorry, June, but it didn't quite make sense to me."

"That's one way of putting it," June replied, before looking over at the school building again as her belly rumbled for a third time. "I'm sorry, Meredith," she added, "but I can't quite think straight. I'm really so very hungry."

***

"We should be able to find something in here," Meredith said as she led June through to the kitchen of Holdham Hall. "I'm sure there's plenty of bread left over from breakfast. At least... I think there should be. We had breakfast this morning, I suppose."

She stopped and looked at the empty benches.

"Sometimes my memory isn't very good," she added.

"Is there no food?" June asked, feeling a flickering sense of dread. "Do I have to wait until lunch?"

"I'm sorry," Meredith said, turning to her. "We could try to ask Mrs. Barker, but I don't think she wants to be disturbed today. Nurse Martha might be able to help, though. We should find her instead. I think she's going to teach some of our classes today."

"I don't want to cause trouble," June told her, only for her belly to rumble again. "It's just that, in my current state, I don't think I'd be able to concentrate on anything. I'd only -"

Hearing footsteps, she turned to see that Alexandra and two other girls were making their way through to join them in the kitchen. She instantly bristled, fully aware that Alexandra usually enjoyed causing trouble, but a moment later she saw that some other girls had followed; indeed, half the school – or more – seemed to have made their way through to the corridor outside the kitchen, and now they stood watching June as her stomach continued to rumble.

"What are you all doing here?" she asked. "Is something wrong?"

"Classes are canceled for today," Alexandra explained, her voice sounding strangely blank.

"Mrs. Barker doesn't seem to be feeling well," one of the other girls added, and she too seemed to be almost in some kind of a daze. "We don't know when she'll be back."

"I see," June replied, struggling to hide the fact that she felt distinctly uneasy. "I don't suppose you know where I might find something to eat, do you? I missed breakfast this morning."

"Why would you want to eat?" Alexandra asked.

"Don't be mean to her!" Meredith called out. "She's new here! She doesn't understand!"

"Then she has to *learn*," Alexandra said, taking a step forward while keeping her gaze fixed very firmly on June's face. "I told you, June, that you shouldn't spend your time with this one. Everyone in the entire school knows that Meredith causes nothing but trouble, but you wouldn't listen, would you? You just thought you knew best."

"I don't want to cause any trouble," June told her. "Do you know where I might find Nurse Martha?"

"She's probably in Mrs. Barker's office."

"Isn't Mrs. Barker in there?"

"I'm really not sure where Mrs. Barker is at

the moment," Alexandra said coldly. "You mustn't keep asking about her. After all, you're the one who upset her."

"I didn't upset anyone," June protested. "At least... I certainly didn't *mean* to upset anyone." She saw several of the other girls stepping up behind Alexandra, and she couldn't help but note that they made for a rather threatening sight. After a moment she instinctively took a step back, while glancing across the kitchen and spotting a door that she hoped would provide a quick escape. "You can really get back to what you were doing, and I'll find Nurse Martha myself or... I'll just keep out of your way."

"You haven't been keeping out of our way very much lately," Alexandra replied. "You've been getting very much *in* our way."

"We've been happy here," another girl added. "Meredith has been causing trouble, but otherwise we've been perfectly happy and we really don't need outsiders coming along and interfering."

"And that's what you are," yet another girl said, stepping out from behind Alexandra. "You're an outsider, and you always will be. You're not welcome here at Holdham Hall."

"Excuse me," June said, hurrying past the counters and heading toward the other door. "I really must -"

Before she could finish, that door opened

and several more girls appeared in view, blocking her way.

"Why do you have to try to ruin everything," one of these new girls asked. "No-one wants you here. No-one asked you to come. You just showed up, even though you were never going to be welcomed."

"I was sent here," June said, backing away as all the girls began to make their way into the kitchen, slowly but surely making their way toward her. "It wasn't even my choice. Mr. Holden was the gentleman who arranged everything, he took charge after my parents died and he said he'd sent girls to Holdham Hall before. He promised me that I'd be looked after here, he told me that Mrs. Barker was a very kind woman. He... I..."

Feeling increasingly uneasy as more and more girls entered the kitchen, June backed away still further, until finally she bumped against the wall. Realizing that she had nowhere else to go, she watched as the girls began to fill the room, forming a wall that kept her from escaping.

"You shouldn't have come back after last night," Alexandra said darkly. "Where's your little suitcase? Did you leave it somewhere?"

"June!" Meredith shouted. "Over here!"

Turning, June saw to her relief that Meredith had found another door. Without stopping to think, she raced over and followed Meredith out into another corridor, before turning and seeing Alexandra's dark, angry stare just as the door slammed shut.

"I don't like them," Meredith said after a moment. "I never have. They scare me."

"Me too," June replied, staring at the closed door and imagining the girls all making their way closer. "I think we need to find Nurse Martha again. She's the only person here who might actually know what's going on." She turned to Meredith. "And she might be able to help us get away from here before it's too late."

CHAPTER NINETEEN

1982...

"MEREDITH, WAIT!" JUNE SHOUTED, as the little girl turned and ran out of sight. "It's me! Come back!"

Rushing out of the dining room, she stopped in the hallway and saw Meredith racing up the stairs.

"Meredith, don't you remember me?" June called out, as tears began to fill her eyes. "I know it's been such a very long time, but it's me, it's June! I'm your friend!"

Stopping, Meredith turned to her. Despite all the years that had passed, the girl hadn't changed at all, and her ghostly figure seemed frozen for a moment as if she didn't quite recognize her visitor.

"Do you remember me?" June asked again, stepping over to the foot of the staircase and looking up at her. "I'm old, aren't I? Well, I'm certainly older than I was last time I was here. Let's see, I was ten years old back then, as were you. We were very precocious, weren't we? People always said that I acted older than my years." She paused, hoping against hope that Meredith would reply. "And now look at me," she continued. "I'm almost fifty years old, can you believe that? And as you can see, I've picked up something of an unusual habit."

She held up the sides of her habit for Meredith to see.

"That was a joke," she added, letting go of the fabric. "I'm sorry. Anyway, the point is, I came back after all these years. I realize now that I should have come back so much sooner. Have you been trapped here all this time? Have you been haunting Holdham Hall, all alone and wondering whether anyone even remembered you?"

Again she waited, but Meredith still showed no sign of a response.

"I never forgot," June continued, as more tears filled her eyes. "Look at you, you haven't changed at all. Not one bit, not since the last time I saw you. It's almost as if you're frozen in time, unable to ever move on. But I'm going to fix that, Meredith. I don't know how, not just yet, but I promise you that I won't leave until you're at peace.

Can you tell me what you want, Meredith? Can you help me to help you?"

"You shouldn't have come back," Meredith replied, her voice sounding cold and distant. "Why do you keep coming back? Why don't you understand?"

"What do you want me to understand?" June asked, worried that Meredith seemed poised to run away at any moment. "I'm here, Meredith. I'm begging you to help me."

"You didn't get it then," she said, looking around as if worried that they were about to be caught at any moment, "and you won't get it now. I'm sorry, June, I tried to help you but you just won't listen!"

Suddenly she turned and raced around the corner, her footsteps quickly disappearing into the distance.

"Wait!" June shouted again, running after her but having trouble taking the stairs too quickly. "Meredith, don't go! Wait for me!"

***

As soon as she reached the door to room thirty, June stopped for a moment to catch her breath. She saw the crack in the wall next to Meredith's old bed, and she felt sure that – having more or less followed the footsteps as they'd intermittently returned – she was now close.

"Meredith?" she gasped, a little shocked by her own lack of fitness. "Are you here? Meredith, I'm sorry, but I'm not quite as spry as I was when we were young. You're going to have to forgive me."

She waited, but a moment later she thought she heard more footsteps in the distance. She turned and looked along the corridor, but already the sound had faded; no longer able to go racing about, she stepped into the room and had to take a seat on one of the beds while she continued to get her breath back.

"I'm getting too old for this," she continued. "You wouldn't believe what I've been up to since I was last here, Meredith." Looking around the room, she wondered whether her old friend was lurking somewhere, and whether she might be able to hear her words. "I've been all over the world," she explained, "and I've seen things that I never would have thought possible."

For a moment she thought back to her various exploits, and finally she shook her head as she felt a growing sense of disbelief.

"Sometimes I wonder whether it's all real," she muttered. "If you could have seen me wading through the snow in Switzerland, or trying to navigate the streets of New York... I only ever wanted a quiet life, yet I have been thrust into something that's far greater than I can comprehend.

Sometimes I worry that I'm being directed by dark forces, but then I remind myself that the Lord would surely not..."

Her voice trailed off as she felt her doubts returning.

"The bear doesn't help," she added, rolling her eyes. "I really don't understand what he's up to, or why he occasionally shows up to nudge me and share a few rather cryptic remarks. He never..."

Before she could finish, she realized that she could hear a voice whispering nearby. She turned and looked around the room, and she quickly focused on the crack; as the whisper continued, June slowly got to her feet, even as she told herself that she might merely be hearing an errant gust of wind. Stepping closer to the crack, however, she realized that the sound most certainly was a voice, and that it seemed to be emerging from the crack's depths.

Turning her head, she put her ear to the crack and listened.

"I know what I saw," Meredith's voice whispered. "I didn't like it at first, but now I know it's true, just like all the other girls said."

"What is?" June replied, keeping her voice low.

"I was so scared when I understood," Meredith continued. "I looked at the window, at the glass, and I saw the ghost. I saw its horrible, scary eyes, and I could tell straightaway that it had been dead for a long time. I've never been so terrified."

"Whose ghost did you see?" June asked. "Was it a woman? Was it someone from this school?"

"She looked so angry," Meredith explained. "I could feel the air getting cold all around me, as if icy fingers were touching my shoulders."

"Was that the ghost?" June replied.

"You don't know what it's like," Meredith whimpered. "You never could have understood, June. Not back then. We were too young, and I tried to warn you at the time but I just couldn't, and the other girls... they were all so horrid."

"The other girls are gone now," June told her. "They -"

"No," she said firmly, interrupting her. "You still don't get it, do you? They're still here, just like they were *always* still here."

"You're not making sense," June murmured, still trying to piece everything together. "You've been alone here for so long, Meredith."

"Not alone."

"What do you mean?"

"I wanted to be alone," Meredith said, sounding more scared than ever now, "but I couldn't find anywhere to hide. Not for long, anyway. They always find me eventually."

"Who are you talking about?" June asked.

"You know their faces."

"I don't," June insisted. "Meredith, you're going to have to forgive me, I'm afraid I'm a rather dim old woman these days. In truth, I don't feel very much cleverer than I was all those years ago, in fact I rather feel as if I'm drowning here. I didn't know at first why I'd been brought back here, Meredith, and to be honest I still don't know exactly what the First Order wanted me to do. But as far as I'm concerned, my one responsibility now is to you, my dearest and oldest friend. I think perhaps I failed you all those years ago, but I'm not going to fail you now and I refuse to leave this place until you're at rest."

She waited to hear Meredith's voice again, as tears ran down her cheeks.

"Tell me what you want," she added finally. "Tell me what you need."

"It's too late," Meredith replied darkly. "I think it's been too late for a very long time."

Before she could reply, June heard footsteps approaching the door, and she turned to see Sister Lucy stepped into view. With a set of papers in her hands, Lucy seemed somewhat nervous, and June couldn't help but notice that her features were rather pale.

"Sister Lucy?" she said, sniffing back tears. "What's wrong?"

"I tallied the names on the gravestone," Lucy replied, and she too had tears in her eyes, "but... Sister June, there's something here that makes absolutely no sense whatsoever. It's the children, the ones who were here all those years ago. What... what year did you say you were at Holdham Hall again?"

"1945," June said with a growing sense of fear in her chest. "Why?"

"That's impossible," Lucy stammered, looking down at the papers again as if she couldn't quite believe what she was seeing, as if she wanted to check and double-check and triple-check all the details. "Sister June... Holdham Hall closed in 1942."

CHAPTER TWENTY

1945...

"PENNY FOR THEM?"

"Hmm?"

Looking up, Peter Holden realized that he'd been staring endlessly at the farthing in his right hand, turning the coin over and over again while lost in thought. Actually, that wasn't quite right; instead he'd been lost in a kind of non-thought, as if he'd been subconsciously trying to empty his mind of all ideas. Now, staring at his wife Susan as she stood in the doorway of their sitting room, he realized that he still couldn't quite shake the sense that something was very wrong.

"Can I get you anything?" Susan asked. "Tea? Something stronger?"

"No, I'm fine, thanks," he replied, getting to his feet and stepping across the room. "At least, I *should* be fine. All my cases are in order. I've got to admit, though, that I can't shake this niggling feeling that I've made a mistake."

"About what?"

Stopping next to her, he paused for a moment.

"Do remember that girl I told you about?" he continued. "I told you about her, didn't I? She's the one who lost her parents. I had to find her somewhere to live in something of a hurry."

"You sent her to that boarding school, didn't you?"

"Usually we try to rehouse the girls with families these days," he admitted. "Places like Holdham Hall tend to seem a little old-fashioned these days, although old Elspeth Barker has always done her best. Still, the department's policy of late has been to always put the girls with a family, so they can be given more individual attention."

"Why didn't you do that with the latest girl?"

"I tried, but I couldn't find anything," he told her. "I was sort of at a bit of a loss, and then I remembered Holdham Hall and I figured that it wouldn't hurt to try the place again. I wrote to Elspeth Barker, telling her that I'd be dropping off another little girl for her school."

"And?" Susan replied. "Is there a problem with that?"

"I've been so busy lately," he continued, "and it's only now that I've realized something a little odd about the whole situation. Susan, you're going to think that I'm terribly careless, but there was so much paperwork and I took over some files from old Roger after he retired, and I suppose somewhere in all of that mess I rather lost track of a few things. And when I was checking again today, I made a rather odd discovery."

"What's that?"

"I wrote to Elspeth Barker," he told her, "but I somehow never noticed that she didn't reply."

"Why wouldn't she reply?"

"It doesn't necessarily mean that anything's wrong," he countered. "I'm not saying that. I've been out of the loop on these cases for a while, you know that, and I suppose I just went back to the methods I used before the war. But I looked through the records, and Roger never sent any girls to Holdham Hall in the past few years, not even the most extreme cases. Why do you think that might be?"

"I don't know," she said, "but it doesn't have to mean anything bad, does it?"

She waited for a reply, but she could tell that her husband was still troubled.

"Well, what did this Elspeth Barker woman

say when you dropped the girl off?" she asked. "Did she give you any reason whatsoever to be concerned?"

"That's just it," he replied. "I'm afraid I was in such a hurry that I've been cutting corners lately. I didn't actually deliver young June to the house myself. Instead I just dropped her off at the gate and told her to find her own way to the house. And now I'm starting to wonder whether I might have made a terrible mistake."

***

"Alright, I'm coming!" the voice called out, as rain crashed down against the porch roof. "Hold your horses. The way you're knocking, anyone'd think the world was about to end."

The door juddered open, revealing the bemused face of Roger Farrier.

"Peter?" he said cautiously as he saw the man standing on his doorstep. "Peter Holden? It's been a while since I've seen you, old fellow. What's -"

"Holdham Hall," Peter said, cutting him off.

"I beg your -"

"I'm sorry to disturb you so late," Peter continued, interrupting yet again, "but it's urgent and I'm afraid I couldn't get through on the telephone. Roger, I need to know why you haven't been sending girls to Holdham Hall over the past few years."

"Roger, shut that door!" Miriam shouted from the back of the house. "You're letting all the heat out!"

"Come inside for a moment," Roger said, gesturing for Peter to enter the hallway, then shutting the door after him. "Sorry, but it's a dastardly night out there, isn't it? The garden needed some rain, though, so I suppose -"

"Roger, I need to know about Holdham Hall," Peter said firmly. "This might be very important."

"We used to send all the stray girls to that place," Roger told him. "I know that might seem careless, but it was a good school. Elspeth Barker was always firm but fair, and I saw for myself how she molded her pupils and turned them into good, honest young women."

"So why did you stop?" Peter asked. "Why didn't you send anyone there after the beginning of 1942?"

"Well, I couldn't."

"Why not?"

"What do you mean?"

"Spit it out, man!" Peter snapped angrily. "We're going round and round in circles here. Why has Holdham Hall not been used for more than three years?"

"Well, because it hasn't been there for more than three years," Roger told him. "Isn't that a little obvious? We couldn't exactly send any girls to an abandoned old school that doesn't have any teachers or pupils there anymore, could we?"

"Abandoned?"

"Since the tragedy," Roger explained, before rolling his eyes. "You must have heard about it."

"I've been away," Peter pointed out. "What happened at Holdham Hall?"

"Oh, it was awful," Roger said, taking a seat on the chair next to the front door. "I don't like to think about all of that, even now. I used to visit the school and see the girls, and they seemed to happy. So carefree. I used to take new girls there, girls who were in a terrible state, and within a year Elspeth Barker would have changed their lives completely. That woman, if you ask me, deserved a medal for all the things she did."

"What happened to them?" Peter asked.

"I can't believe you don't know already," Roger replied. "It was all over the news at the time, but I suppose you were off in the war. They say the girls were all sent to shelter in one of the rooms of the place, and that's where they all were on that awful night. The Germans used to drop any leftover bombs, you see, and they didn't really care where they landed. I'm sure they weren't specifically aiming for a school, but one of those bombs just fell right on top of it. I suppose, if you think about it, at least that means it would've been quick. All the pupils would have died instantly."

***

"Peter, where are you going?" Roger shouted, struggling to be heard above the rain as he watched Peter hurrying toward his car. "What's wrong?"

"I should never have been so stupid," Peter muttered, fumbling in his pockets for his notebook, only to lose his grip and drop it onto the path. "What was I thinking?"

"Peter, what's going on?" Roger asked.

"I dropped a girl off at Holdham Hall," he said, picking the notebook up and turning to his former colleague. "A young girl, a couple of days ago. This mess is completely my fault, I'm not trying to blame anyone else, but I have to rectify the problem immediately."

"Wait a moment," Roger replied, "are you seriously saying that she's been there at that old school for days? All by herself?"

"I just have to hope that she's alright," Peter said, clearly in a state of panic. "It's about two hours to Holdham Hall from here. If I hurry, I might be able to get there by midnight."

"Hang on," Roger said, reaching back into the porch before pulling his jacket out. "I'm going to come with you. I'm sure everything's okay, but just in case it's not, two heads are always better than one."

"Get a move on, then," Peter replied, heading to his car and climbing into the driver's seat. "God only knows what poor June's been getting up to, stranded for so long at that school all alone."

CHAPTER TWENTY-ONE

WITH RAIN BATTERING THE windows and darkness having fallen outside, June slowly pushed open the door to Mrs. Barker's office. She wasn't entirely sure what to expect, but to her surprise she saw Nurse Martha sitting at the desk, leafing through some paperwork.

"What is it?" Meredith whispered, having hung back a little. "June? What do you see?"

"Ah, there you are," Martha said with a smile, glancing at June briefly before returning her attention to the papers. "I've rather lost track of today, if I'm honest. You were missing from class this morning, June. I was covering for Mrs. Barker and I noticed your absence. I didn't make a big deal of it, but I have to admit, I'm curious. Where were you?"

"Nowhere," June said cautiously, stepping into the room with Meredith a few paces behind. "I just think -"

Before she could finish, her belly gurgled loudly.

"You seem hungry," Martha pointed out.

"Please, if it's okay, might I have some food?" June asked. "I somehow seem to have missed every meal since I got here. There's always been some reason, and now I'm starving."

"Starving?"

"I got some water," June continued, "although the pipes here seem a little old and dirty. But I'm so hungry, I can barely even think properly."

"Well, we should do something about that," Martha replied merrily. "Have you been to the kitchen and asked the cook for some leftovers?"

"There was nobody there," June told her.

"Wasn't there?" Martha looked at June, who stopped on the other side of the desk. "Oh, no," she continued, "I suppose that's right. The cook was dear old Mildred, and she was with us all in the main hall when..." Her voice trailed off for a moment. "That was a terrible night, you know. We were sheltering, just like we'd sheltered so many times before, and I suppose in some ways we'd become a little careless. We were supposed to be operating a strict blackout, but we might have let a little light out. In fact, I think I might have been the one who left a candle burning at one of the windows. You wouldn't think that'd be enough, would you? One little candle, in one little window? It's hard to believe that a pilot up there would be able to see such a thing, even on the darkest night. Then again, perhaps he didn't. Perhaps it was just a coincidence."

She paused, before holding up a faded old envelope.

"Somebody sent a letter announcing your arrival," she explained, before setting it down and holding up a framed photograph. "This is a picture that was taken of the girls shortly before the accident. If you look closely, you can see that I've pasted a picture of you over the face of a girl who left a few days before... well, before all the bad things happened. There was a small photograph of you with the letter, and by chance it fitted rather well. I think I shall hang this back in the hallway, near the stairs. That would be nice, don't you think? It would show that you fit in here."

"I don't know what you're talking about," June said as her belly rumbled again. "Please, can I just have some food? I'm so hungry." She turned to Meredith. "You're hungry too, aren't you?"

"I don't know," Meredith replied, furrowing her brow for a moment. "I suppose so. I mean... not really."

"Well, *I* am," June continued, turning to Martha. "I don't even mind what it is. I'm not fussy."

"Let's try to sort things out," Martha said, getting to her feet and stepping around the desk, then holding a hand out toward June. "Come on, we'll go together to the main hall. There's something there that I want to show you."

"Is there food?"

"Trust me," Martha continued, reaching closer and taking June's hand. "I never thought this opportunity would arise. Now that it has, I really don't want to waste it." She squeezed June's hand a little tighter. "Oh, you're so nice and warm. It's been so long since I felt a warm hand."

***

"I don't think I've been to this part of the school before," June said as she followed Martha along a dark corridor, with Meredith trailing further behind. "Where are we going?"

"I've tended to keep this part closed off," Martha told her. "I find that's better for the girls. There's no point in upsetting them by reminding them of unpleasant things. The window does enough of that."

"What do you mean?" June asked.

"Nurse Martha?" Meredith said suddenly,

stopping in her tracks. "I don't feel well."

Martha turned to her.

"I feel scared," Meredith continued, looking past her and watching the darkness ahead. "I don't know why, but I feel like something scary's crawling through my tummy."

"Then by all means go back and find the other girls," Martha told her. "I should have said that sooner, really. Go on, Meredith, you'll probably be much happier with them. What I have to show June is... best kept for her eyes only."

"I'll be okay," June added, as her belly rumbled yet again. "Or are you hungry?"

"No," Meredith replied, turning and hurrying back the way they'd come. "I'm sorry, June. Please forgive me!"

"For what?" June asked, before Martha pulling on her hand, forcing her to start walking again. "Why did Meredith say that just now? What did she mean?"

"Don't put too much stock in childish nonsense," Martha replied with a smile. "You know, June, you're very special here. I'm sure I said this to you before, but you're really not like the other girls." She squeezed her hand again. "I never really thought that I'd get this chance. Deep down, I know that what happened that night was my fault. The pain, the horror, the terrible noise... I was the only survivor, and I tried so hard to make things right. I took the girls outside, one by one, and I buried them. I couldn't always be sure which girl was which, some of them were so badly hurt that their body parts were like chunks of meat. I think I did alright, though. I mean, I must have done. When the police turned up, and the authorities got involved, they agreed to let the bodies rest in peace."

"What bodies?" June asked, spotting a door up ahead. "I don't know what you mean. Nurse Martha, I really just want something to eat."

"I stayed on to atone for my sins," Martha continued. "It was all I could do, really. And when I started to see the girls again, at first I assumed that I was losing my mind. Then Mrs. Barker came back as well, and I realized that perhaps a miracle had been granted. Of course, the girls were easy to fool, whereas Mrs. Barker began to notice that something was wrong, and she started to lose her mind. And then, eventually, something unbelievably wonderful happened." Stopping at the door, she reached out for the handle. "You arrived, June. I hid for a while, I didn't dare come to you, I assumed there had been a dreadful mistake. But now I see that it wasn't a mistake at all. You were sent by some higher power, to give me another chance."

She tried to turn the handle, only for it to stick a little.

"Hold on one moment," she added. "It's like this sometimes. I think the wall buckled very slightly when the bomb hit, but I can usually jiggle it."

"Please, Nurse Martha," June whimpered, "I'm so hungry."

"I can find you something later," Martha said, still struggling with the handle. "I've been catching rabbits and squirrels in the forest and eating those. They're really not so bad, not once you get used to them. I've also been eating some mushrooms that grow out there. Those sting a little on the tongue and they sometimes make me feel very peculiar." She looked down and smiled at June. "Sometimes, after eating them, I see the most amazing shapes and colors in the air. You will too, if you're lucky. And then -"

Before she could finish, the handle budged and the door creaked open.

"Ah, perfect," she whispered, with a hint of anticipation in her voice. "I probably should have showed you this earlier, June, but I was struggling to work out exactly what to do with you. I didn't think about the food thing, I suppose that slipped my mind. I'm so used to the other girls here just... managing."

She pulled on June's hand, forcing her to follow her through the doorway.

"I still feel very sad whenever I come in here," she added. "I just really don't like thinking about the tragedy of that night."

June opened her mouth to ask what she meant, but in that moment she saw the awful truth. She looked into what remained of a large hall, but the ceiling had been shattered and debris cover the floor, while parts of the far wall had collapsed as well, leaving a view of the starry sky above. Looking round the vast area, June saw a scene of utter devastation, and a moment later a gust of cold wind blew against her face.

"Welcome to the hall of Holdham Hall," Martha said, as moonlight caught her wide-open, glaring eyes. "This is where everything changed on that awful night. This is where the bomb landed while all the girls were supposed to be safe."

CHAPTER TWENTY-TWO

"WHAT BOMB?" JUNE STAMMERED, taking a step forward as she continued to look around, still trying to understand the sheer enormity of so much destruction. "What happened here?"

"I'd just popped out," Martha replied, as tears welled in her eyes. "We had a policy of getting all the girls to shelter in here if we thought there was any danger. We'd all gathered, and then I remembered the candle in my room. I came to the door and rushed out, telling Mrs. Barker that I needed to check something, and then..."

Her voice trailed off as she remembered the immense explosion, and the force that her knocked her off her feet.

"It wasn't a direct hit, exactly," she continued. "That would have destroyed most of the school. It was just enough to make the ceiling come down, and all that stone and masonry fell on the girls, crushing them to death. The lucky ones died instantly, but a few were left screaming in agony as they died. I tended to them as best I could, trying to save them in the moonlight, but eventually I realized that the most humane thing to do... I didn't have anything to hand that I could use, so I reasoned that I simply had to work quickly. I took a brick and I smashed their skulls, each of them one by one until they were all dead. The last few had seen what I was doing, they begged me for mercy, but they didn't realize that mercy was *exactly* what I was giving them?"

June hesitated, before hearing a shuffling sound nearby. Turning, she saw Mrs. Barker on her knees, sobbing next to the rubble.

"Elspeth was the last survivor," Martha explained, as she too watched the weeping woman. "Her legs were mangled, but she probably would have made it, but she just couldn't handle what I'd done. She told me I'd been wrong, that I should have tried harder to save some of the girls. She just wouldn't stop going on and on about the fact that I'd killed the survivors, and I told her to shut up but she wouldn't listen. She was screaming, she'd entirely lost her mind, so I showed her mercy too. And then, when they all came back as ghosts, I helped Elspeth focus on the children once more. That plan worked until you showed up."

June turned to Martha again.

"I think, deep down, she immediately knew that you were different," Martha told her. "Elspeth Barker was always a good woman, but the horror of that night changed her, and in death that final madness remained. Her whip was always just a deterrent, she'd never used it before, but when she struck you with it... I think she was driven completely out of her mind by the sight of the blood that came from your back. By the flesh. By the realization that you were actually alive. I've tried to talk to her since, but she's just a terrible mess. At least she's here, where the girls hopefully won't find her. I suppose I shall have to take over their teaching until she feels better."

"I want to leave," June said, turning and hurrying to the door, only for Martha to grab her arm and hold her tight. "Please, I just want to go."

"You'll tell people," Martha sneered. "About the fact that I came back here, and about the ghosts. You might even tell them what I just admitted to you, which isn't... quite the official story."

"You're hurting me!" June shouted, trying to pull free from her grip.

"I'm going to show you mercy," Martha continued. "Do you know what your problem has been since you first arrived here, June? You haven't been able to fit in with the other girls. You're too different. But that's okay, because there's a very easy way to fix that problem. We're just going to have to make you a lot more like them." She tightened her grip as June tried again to break free. "You'll thank me later, June. Just like the rest of them thank me now. You won't be scared again, and you won't ever feel hunger."

"Help me!" June yelled, even though she knew there was no-one in earshot who might rush to her aid. "Please! I need help!"

"I'll make it quick and painless," Martha told her. "It'll be much quicker than -"

Suddenly June twisted free, dropping to her knees in the process but immediately scrambling to her feet and racing out through the door.

"You won't get far!" Martha shouted after her. "June, why are you prolonging this? Come back and let me show you the mercy you so richly deserve!"

***

"Help!" June screamed, racing along the corridor and rushing back into the kitchen. "Somebody -"

Stopping suddenly, she saw all the other pupils standing on front of her. This time, however, something was different; the girls were all glaring at her, but June could see strange shadows around their eyes, as if their features had begun to shrink deeper into the recesses of their skulls, as if death was starting to show through their features. She told herself that she had to be wrong, but as a few of the girls stepped forward June realized that they seemed strangely discolored, almost rotten.

"We warned you last night," Alexandra snarled, as patches of dead flesh began to spread across her face. "Why didn't you listen to us when we warned you at the graves?"

"That was you?" June stammered.

"Most of the time we forget the worst parts," Alexandra continued. "I was one of the last to die. I saw Sister Martha coming toward me with that brick, I saw the blood all over it and the parts of other girls' brains. I begged her to let me live, I told her it was only my leg that was hurt, but she insisted on being merciful. I don't think about that moment too much, though, not unless someone like you brings it up again. I prefer to just get on with my days and nights here at the school. We're all the same like that."

"I don't want to be here," June told her, struggling to hold back tears. "Please, I just want to leave."

"You can't leave," Martha said, stepping up behind her and grabbing her by the shoulder. "Not now that you're ready to become one of them. Just let me make a few cuts here and there, and we'll get rid of all that nasty blood that's keeping you alive."

"No!" June shouted, pulling away and rushing across the kitchen, slipping past the other girls and racing out into the hallway. "Help!"

Racing to the front door, she grabbed the handle and struggled to pull it open. The door was large and heavy, but she just about managed to create a gap before running out onto the lawn at the front of the school. A fraction of a second later, however, Martha grabbed her from behind and pulled her back, and they tumbled down together onto the grass. Before June could even try to get up, however, Martha scrambled on top, straddling her and holding her down with one hand while placing her other hand around her throat.

"You wouldn't make it easy, would you?" she snarled. "I'm sorry, June, but if you're anything like the other girls, you won't remember much of this once you're on the other side. The pain will only be temporary. Everything else will be eternal."

She began to squeeze tight, before taking the broken brick from her pocket and holding it up high, ready to bring it crashing down against June's skull.

"We're all one big happy family here at Holdham Hall," she continued, "and -"

Before she could get another word out, they were both picked out by a set of bright headlights. Looking along the road, June and Martha saw a car racing closer, before the vehicle screeched to a halt and two figures quickly climbed out.

"June!" Mr. Holden shouted. "Get over here!"

"Leave us alone!" Martha screamed, as he and Roger began to approach. "I won't tell you twice! Something awful happened here, but I've fixed it and now everything's alright again. You just have to leave us alone! All of you! The whole world has to stay away!"

"Let her go," Mr. Holden said, holding his hands up as he edged closer. "Whatever's going on here, we can sort it all out. There's no need to harm the child."

"Turn those lights off!" Martha yelled, staring directly at the headlights of the car. "Are you insane? There's supposed to be a blackout! If you don't turn them off, the Germans will see them and drop another bomb!"

"Germans?" Roger said cautiously. "What are you talking about? The war's over, there's no -"

"Leave us alone!" Martha shouted again, before bringing the broken brick crashing down against the side of June's head. "You've got no right to be here! Leave us alone and don't ever come back!"

CHAPTER TWENTY-THREE

1982...

"CLOSED?" JUNE SAID, REACHING up and touching the side of her head for a moment as she struggled to understand what was happening. "In 1942? No, that's impossible, I was here three years later."

"I really don't see how you could have been," Lucy told her, still standing in the doorway and looking into room thirty. "Sister June, I don't mean to be too curious, but I must ask... exactly how much do you remember of your time here at Holdham Hall?"

"I remember being dropped off at the end of the road by a nice gentleman named Mr. Holden," June said, wincing as she felt a flicker of pain in her head, "and I had to walk to the front door."

"And then what happened?"

"Mrs. Barker greeted me," June explained, "and I met the other girls. Something was a little strange, though, because I remember no-one fed me. I was so hungry, I was starving by the second or third day. I went to find some food, Mrs. Barker had fallen ill or..."

Her voice trailed off as she tried to remember.

"I *think* she was ill," she added, and now she sounded increasingly uncertain. "There was someone else here, though, a woman who took over our lessons. Not that we had many lessons, in truth, because everything was so confusing and -"

"How long did you spend at Holdham Hall?" Lucy asked, interrupting her.

"A matter of months," June said, before hesitating. "Or was it even that long? Weeks, perhaps, or -"

"Or just a few days?"

"I don't know why it's so difficult to remember the details," June continued, swallowing hard. "To be honest with you, I'm feeling rather light-headed now." She made her way over to the door, but she had to reach out after a moment and support herself against the wall. "Why are the details so vague?" she murmured. "There another member of staff here, another woman. I think she might have been a nun."

"What was her name?"

"Didn't I mention her earlier?"

"Did you?"

"Sister Martha," June said after a moment, before letting out a sigh of relief. "Yes, that's right, there was a nun here named Sister Martha. She was a kind of assistant, and a nurse too. I think she stepped in whenever Mrs. Barker needed help."

"Do you remember anything else about her?" Lucy asked. "Sister June, this paperwork really doesn't match up with what you've told me, but there's another problem. The names on some of the graves match the names of the girls who were here in 1942 when the school closed, and the number of graves matches exactly. I think all the pupils died and that's why the school shut and -"

"Wait!" June gasped, as she heard footsteps in the distance. Pushing past Lucy, she stumbled out into the corridor and looked toward the top of the stairs. "Meredith," she called out, "it's me! Meredith, wait! I need to know the truth!"

***

A few minutes later, after hurrying down the stairs, June made her way through to the dining room and stopped as soon as she spotted Meredith's ghostly figure standing at the far end, staring out through the glass at the bottom of the sixth window.

"Meredith," she said, her voice tense with fear as Sister Lucy stopped right behind her, "it's me. Please, don't run away again. I only want to help."

Ignoring Sister Lucy, she made her way over, and this time to her immense relief Meredith stayed in place. Staring at the clear glass frame at the bottom of the window, Meredith seemed to be lost in thought, as if she'd barely even noticed June's arrival at all.

"I'm so sorry that you were left alone here for so long," June told her. "I'd like to set that right, if I can."

"I can see it," Meredith whispered, still staring at the window.

"What can you see?"

"I can see a ghost."

"Where?"

June moved behind her and crouched down so that she could see Meredith's view of the glass, but she was unable to properly make out anything on the lawn.

"I don't see anyone," she told Meredith after a few seconds. "The glass is so warped, how can you tell who's out there at all?"

"Not out there," Meredith replied, reaching up and tapping the glass. "In here."

"What do you -"

Before she could finish, June realized that she could just about make out a hint of not only her own reflection in the glass, but Meredith's face as well. In the reflected image, Meredith's features were very different, with dark shadows around her dead eyes.

"I'm dead," Meredith continued, raising her voice a little. "I remember now. We're all dead, all of us. We died on that awful night. Some of us were killed when the bomb hit, and some of us... I remember Sister Martha going around, showing us all mercy."

"Your voice travels through the crack," June said, looking at the crack in the wall as she began to understand. "Any girl who sees a ghost in this window is merely seeing her own dead reflection, and her voice carried to room thirty and probably to other rooms as well. That's how the other girls end up here, and they see the reflection as well. They remember, albeit briefly, that they're dead. The rest is just a mangled childhood superstition."

"I didn't want to die," Meredith sobbed. "I wanted to be alive for a long time. I wanted to grow up and be an adult, like you." She turned and looked up at June. "Why couldn't I do that? Why did someone I never met drop a bomb that killed us all?"

"I'm afraid that sort of thing happens in war sometimes," June told her, and now she too was once again struggling to hold back tears. "All these decades later, it *still* happens. It's so very wrong, and I pray for the souls of anyone who loses their life, but I don't know how -"

"It shouldn't happen," Meredith replied, interrupting her. "It's not fair."

"I know it's not fair," June continued, "but -"

"I don't want to be dead!" Meredith screamed, lunging at her. "I want to be alive!"

Shocked, June pulled back against the wall. She raised her hands to defend herself, but in that moment Meredith faded from sight. Suddenly feeling her legs starting to buckle, June began to slide down onto the floor, before Sister Lucy rushed over and held her up.

"You must sit down," Lucy said, helping her over to the nearest chair. "There you go. It's all going to be alright."

"Did you see her?" June asked with tears running down her face.

"I did," Lucy replied, "but let us focus on you right now." Reaching into her pocket, she took out a few items, one of which was a handkerchief. She set a couple of small books on the table, before dabbing at June's eyes. "There we go," she continued, "it'll all be better soon."

"Wait," June said, picking up the books and looking at them, seeing the name of St.

Gwendoline's Convent on their fronts. "Are you..." She stared at the text, and then she looked up into Lucy's face. "Are you *really* a nun?"

"I told you," Lucy said with a faint, slightly sad half-smile. "Why would I lie?"

"But your glasses -"

"I told you, I thought I'd left them behind and then I found that I hadn't." She paused, clearly puzzled. "Sister June, is everything quite alright?"

"You're actually a nun," June said, leaning back in the chair as she let out a sigh of relief. "I'm so dreadully sorry, Sister Lucy, I suppose over the years I've come to suspect anyone and anything. I must take care to not be so judgmental in the future."

"That's quite alright," Lucy replied.

"It's not," June muttered, shaking her head. "After all this madness, the fact that you're exactly what you say you are, that you're truly a nun... that seems almost to be the biggest twist of all."

"Well, I shall take that as a compliment," Lucy said, stepping over to the other end of the table and pouring some water from a jug into some glasses. "I think you might need this," she added. "It's been standing out since breakfast, but I don't suppose that's too bad."

"Lord, forgive me for my suspicious mind," June said, looking up at the ceiling. "I shall endeavor to be a better person from now on."

"I've been a nun for a while now," Lucy continued.

"A most pleasant way of life," June observed, trying to have a normal conversation for once.

"I do so greatly value the peace I derive from my work at the convent."

"As do I."

"I must admit, I also enjoy running little events for the local community."

"A worthy cause," June suggested.

"I was actually sent to live with the sisters of St. Gwendoline's at a very young age," Lucy continued, turning to her. "I moved down south later for a while, but I missed St. Gwendoline's so much that I went back. St. Gwendoline's has always felt like my real home. Almost from birth, actually. That would have been back in 1946." She paused, holding the glass of water but making no attempt to take it over to June. "My mother couldn't look after me, you see," she added, fixing June with a dark, determined stare. "She was in no fit state to look after anyone, including herself. She was born in an asylum, after... well, let's just say that some very bad things had happened to her by the time she gave birth to me."

CHAPTER TWENTY-FOUR

1945...

"NO!" MARTHA SCREAMED, STRUGGLING to get free as four men – one holding each limb – carried her away from Holdham Hall and toward a waiting ambulance. "Get off me! You can't do this! I haven't done anything wrong!"

"She's out of her bloody mind," Sergeant McDonough said with a sigh as he watched the woman being loaded into the ambulance. "She bit one of my officers when he tried to subdue her."

"Where's the girl she was found with?" Sergeant Leeds asked.

"She's been taken to the hospital already," McDonough explained. "She got quite a whack to the head, but probably nothing too serious. I'm sure she'll be fine." Looking at the ambulance again, he saw that his men were struggling to load the struggling woman into the back. "This lady, on the other hand, clearly has some quite serious mental issues. If you ask me, she needs locking up in a padded cell, and I wouldn't have thought she'll be out again in a hurry."

"Has she really been living here all alone for years?" Leeds replied, turning to look at Holdham Hall again. "I remember when this place got hit by that bomb. Such a tragedy."

"There was no-one else here until recently," McDonough observed, "although..."

His voice trailed off as, for a moment, he thought he saw something moving in the shadows near the front door. He heard a giggling sound, as if children were playing, but that sound quickly faded to nothing. A few seconds later, before he had a chance to say anything, he heard a cry of pain. He turned just in time to see that Martha had broken free and was running away across the lawn, with three officers already chasing after her while the fourth clutching a wound on his arm.

"She bit me!" the injured man gasped. "The mad bitch actually bit me!"

"Should we go and help them catch her?" Leeds asked.

"They're younger than us, they should be fine," McDonough muttered, before patting his belly. "I don't know about you, but my running days are in the past." He watched as Martha disappeared between the trees, following by the officers. "They'll nab her. Hell, it might even be a blessing in disguise if they have to chase her down first. If she's tired out by all that running, she'll hopefully be less trouble once we get her into the ambulance."

***

"Let go of me!" Martha shouted, still struggling several hours later as she was carried through the large open doorway that led into Bendel Asylum's main ward. "You don't understand what you're doing!"

"Cell nine for her," Carter, the lead warden, muttered as he led the way. "Doctor Finnegan won't be able to see her until Monday. He's supposed to be on duty over the weekend, but there's a big golf game he has to attend so..."

Reaching cell nine, he stopped for a moment to unlock the door, before pulling it aside and watching as Martha was carried past.

"She's a feisty one, I'll give her that," he commented with a grin. "I like it when they arrive like that. Makes them feel like more of a project, somehow."

"I have to get back to Holdham Hall!" Martha screamed. "You're making a terrible mistake! The girls need me! What will they do if I'm not there?"

"Any idea what she's going on about?" one of the orderlies asked, sounding a little breathless as he helped attach Martha's wrist to a manacle on the wall. "All the way in here, she kept rambling about some girls."

"Beats me," Carter replied, watching as Martha kicked in vain against the staff. "Sounds like the mad cries of a deranged woman who lost her mind."

"They're there because of me," Martha stammered, pulling on the metal cuff around her wrist, trying to break it free from its mounting point on the wall. "It's my fault that this happened to them, but I can still make it alright. I just have to go to them again and help them to understand that they're dead. They only realize when they see their own reflections, and then they forget as soon as they're away from the window."

Carter raised one eyebrow, clearly amused by her claims.

"I can care for them!" Martha yelled. "Why can't any of you see that? I was okay there, I was looking after them and we were all happy! Why did people have to come and ruin it?"

"What do you want us to do now?" one of the orderlies asked, stepping back from Martha as she continued to pull on the manacle. "She clearly needs to be sedated."

"I'll sort that out later," Carter said, keeping his eyes fixed very firmly on Martha. "The rest of you head back to the office and see about checking on our other guests."

"But -"

"I'll finish dealing with this fine young lady," he sneered. "I mean it. I want time alone with her."

"Fine," the orderly said, as he and the other men made their way out of the cell. "You're welcome to her. Apparently she bit a couple of the police officers who were arresting her. If you ask me, women like her are little more than animals. She's vermin, and she oughta be treated that way."

"You might have a point," Carter replied, shutting the cell door once they were gone, leaving him alone with Martha. "I've got to admit," he added as he stepped over to her, "we've had a lot of people come to stay with us here at Bendel over the years, but you're the very first nun."

"Get me out of here!" she hissed, lunging at him, only for the manacle to hold her back. "Why are you interfering like this?"

"You've been a naughty girl, Martha," he said with a grin. "How old are you, anyway? Late twenties? Don't you think you should have learned how to behave by now?" He stepped closer and looked down at her as she remained on her knees on the floor. "It's not your fault. Someone should have taken you in hand a long time ago, and shown you the ropes."

"Go to Hell!" she snapped.

"I already *work* in Hell," he replied. "Welcome, by the way. I'm sure you're really going to like it here once the doctors get started with their treatment. Tomorrow we'll shave you all over, and I mean every little nook and cranny, just to make sure you don't get lice. Then -"

Before he could finish, Martha spat at him. Flinching, Carter wiped the blob of spit from his cheek, and then he smacked the side of Martha's face so hard that she cried out as she fell back.

"Okay," he snarled, as he began to undo his belt, before unzipping his trousers, "clearly you've got a little too much fight in you. That's alright, though. I know a surefire way to change your mind. Although, seeing as how you're a nun, I'm going to hazard a guess that it involves doing something you've never done before! You should relax, though. Some women even enjoy it."

***

Nine months later, Martha tilted her head back and screamed. Her hair was short, and bloodied sweat covered her face as another contraction burst through her body. Struggling for breath, she leaned back against the bed, squeezing her eyes tight shut until finally she heard the cries of her newborn baby.

"Let me see!" she gasped, opening her eyes and trying to sit up, only to immediately feel a rush of weakness.

Blinking furiously, she tried to clear her blurred vision. She could see the doctor holding a squirming, screaming child, and she watched as the nurse made her way over to cut the umbilical cord. Instinctively Martha reached out to take her child, only for the handcuffs to keep her wrists securely fastened to the metal railings on either side of the bed.

"Give him to me!" she stammered. "Please, I want to see him!"

"It's a girl," the nurse replied, turning to her.

"That's enough," the doctor reminded her. "It's policy here not to give the patients any information that might upset them."

"What about the father?" the nurse asked. "If the patient has been here for nine months, then -"

"Carter was moved on months ago," the doctor said, turning and carrying the crying child toward the door. "No-one minded him having his way with a few of the inmates, but he got greedy and eventually people talked. Finnegan pulled some strings and had him moved over to St. Michael's

Hospital on the other side of town."

"St. Michael's?" the nurse replied, turning to him. "Isn't that a children's hospital?"

"Clean up here," the doctor said firmly. "I'm going to go and find those women who came to take the baby. They've promised to give it a good life at some convent or other. It'll certainly have a better chance than it would with this lousy excuse for a mother."

"Bring her back!" Martha screamed, trying again to get up from the bed. "She's my baby! Give her to me!"

"Don't struggle too much," the nurse replied calmly. "We just need to clean you up a little, and then you can go back to your cell. And then, if you ask me, your best bet is just to pretend that none of this ever happened."

"Bring her back!" Martha shouted again, at the top of her voice, as she imagined her newborn daughter being carried away along the corridor. "I'm her mother! You have to bring her back to me!"

CHAPTER TWENTY-FIVE

1982...

"BY THE TIME I managed to find the records with her name," Lucy continued, staring intently at June, "it was too late. She'd died not long after I was born. Suicide, the doctors said. She wrapped a sheet around her neck in her cell and... apparently she never stopped hearing the cries of the dying children."

"I'm not entirely sure that I follow," June said cautiously, still sitting at the far end of the table in Holdham Hall's dining room. "Your mother -"

"My mother was a good woman," Lucy replied, cutting her off as the first trace of anger reached her voice. "Not like my father. He died in prison, but he should have hung after the awful things he did at that children's hospital. I don't care about him, but my mother was perfect. She was a saint." She began to make her way toward June, walking slowly and with purpose. "She never should have been dragged away from here, but people had to interfere. Outsiders had to come to Holdham Hall. A stupid little child had to come and ruin it all."

Stopping, she looked down at June.

"Do you even remember my mother?" she added.

"I remember a woman," June stammered, staring back up at her. "It's all so vague, but I think there was another woman here. A kind woman, a woman named Martha who -"

"That's her," Lucy said, interrupting her. "That was my mother. A good woman who made one mistake many years ago, and who tried to fix that mistake by looking after all the children even after they'd died. She would have given her entire life to them, if only she'd been allowed to stay here. If only *you*, June, hadn't come along and got in the way."

"I was dropped off here," June replied, trying to get to her feet, only for Lucy to put a hand on her shoulder and force her back down into the chair. "I think so, at least. It's so vague and I'm struggling to recall the details."

"How convenient," Lucy sneered. "You cost my mother everything. If it wasn't for you turning up all those years ago, no-one else would ever have come knocking. If they had, they wouldn't have thought there was anything amiss. But because of you, June, my mother got into a lot of trouble. It's your fault that she ended up killing herself in that hospital cell."

"No," June said, shaking her head, "please, you have to understand, I was just a child, I was only doing what I was told. I didn't even -"

Before she could get another word out, she saw that Lucy was now holding part of a broken brick.

"I don't know," Lucy snarled, "if this is the exact same brick my mother used when she tried to kill you thirty-seven years ago, but it was out the front so there's definitely a chance." She held it up. "There's a slight stain on the side, that might be blood or it might not." She turned the brick around so that June could see the darkened patch. "Do you remember this finally? It has been so frustrating listening to your feeble attempts to remember exactly what happened to you all those years ago. You're really quite thick sometimes, Sister June."

She raised the brick higher still, ready to bring it crashing back down. "When the First Order offered me a chance to finish what my mother started all those years ago, I'm afraid something inside me just broke. Why, I don't think there's a soul in the world who'd be able to resist this change of revenge."

With that, she slammed the brick down against June, who could only cry out and pull back. At the very last second, however, a ghostly figure lunged at Lucy, pushing her away.

"Leave her alone!" Meredith screamed as the brick fell to the floor. "June! Run!"

Scrambling to her feet, June hurried away from the chair and past the table. Her mind was racing as memories began to flood back, and as she reached the doorway and turned to see Lucy hauling herself up from the floor.

"Run!" Meredith screamed again. "Get away from her while you still have a chance!"

Rushing from the room, June headed to the large front door, only to find when she pulled on the handle that it was locked. She tried a couple more times before turning to see that Lucy was limping after her; running away from the door, June made her way past the foot of the staircase and through into the kitchen, almost tripping on the steps and only just managing to keep from falling. She hurried past the old benches, vaguely aware that she'd been chased through the same part of the school before, and finally she tumbled through the nearest door she could find, stopping as she looked ahead and saw Mrs. Barker's desk.

And...

"Mrs. Barker?" she stammered, seeing the old headmistress sitting behind the desk once more. "How..."

"What do you want?" Mrs. Barker snapped, looking up at her and then staring for a moment. "Now, who are you and what are you doing at my school? We already have Sister Martha and -"

Stopping suddenly, she seemed momentarily confused, before slowly getting to her feet.

"Young June," she added cautiously, her voice trembling with shock now. "You're much older than before, but I recognize you even after all these years. It *is* you, is it not?"

"I don't want to cause any trouble," June replied, before hearing footsteps rushing closer. Turning, she saw that Lucy was hurrying across the kitchen. "Please, I didn't even want to come here in the first place!"

Slamming the door, she slid the bolt across just in time, before Lucy could force it open again. As she stepped back, June heard Lucy throwing herself against the door again and again, causing it to shudder loudly in its frame. After a few more seconds, however, the sound stopped and June heard the footsteps racing away again.

"She's going to find another way through," she stammered, before turning to Mrs. Barker again. "What do I -"

In that instant, Mrs. Barker's whip cracked against June, catching the side of her face and sending her crumpling to the floor. Just about managing to stay on her hands and knees, June winced as she saw a few drops of blood falling from the cut on her cheek, and then she looked up to see Mrs. Barker towering above her.

"Blood," the older woman snarled. "I remember it like it was yesterday. I tried to punish you the way I punished the other girls, but you... you actually bled! That was when I realized you weren't like the rest of them, it was then I realized that you'd come here from the outside world. Until that moment I was confused, I assumed you were just another ghost I'd forgotten, but when I saw the blood... I realized that the outside world was finally going to come and disturb us again."

Sniffing back tears, she raised the whip higher.

"I can't have that reminder here at Holdham

Hall. Sister Martha was bad enough, but at least she had the good sense to mostly stay out of the way, whereas you... I only want to look after the children. Why can't anyone see that? I just want to look after them forever and make sure they're not scared!"

She brought the whip cracking down, but this time June just about managed to scramble out of the way, crawling toward the far side of the room before stumbling to her feet. She pulled the other door open and stepped out into the corridor; once she was sure that there was no sign of Sister Lucy, she turned to see that Mrs. Barker was making her way closer with the whip still in her hand.

"You will stay here and face your punishment!" Mrs. Barker snarled angrily. "Then, when you're like the rest of the girls, I shall perhaps find a way to make you happy!"

"Leave me alone!" June shouted, swinging the door shut and taking a step back, then realizing that she could no longer hear any sound of movement in the office. "I'm sorry," she continued, realizing that Elspeth Barker had been driven mad – both in life and in death – by the horrific way that the children had died. "I'm so sorry. I hope you find peace."

Turning, she hurried along the next corridor, then the next, desperately trying to find a way out of the building. She was less familiar with this part of Holdham Hall, only vaguely recognizing the various rooms, and for a few minutes she felt utterly and completely lost. Trying not to panic, she raced from corridor to corridor, until finally she spotted a large wooden door that seemed slightly familiar. Hurrying over, she struggled for a moment to get the door open, finding that it seemed slightly warped in its frame; finally she succeeded, swinging it open and hurrying through, only to stop in her tracks as she saw a place that was both new and horribly familiar at the same time.

Looking around, she found herself staring once again – after so many years – into the collapsed main hall of the old school. Rubble covered most of the floor, marking the spots where so many children had died when the bomb hit. Above, stars could be seen shining brightly in the night sky as June stepped out across the shattered space, and now she finally remembered that she'd been there so many years earlier with Sister Martha.

"Well," Sister Lucy said suddenly, forcing June to spin round and see her standing in the doorway, "this seems appropriate. I think the time has finally come to finish what my mother started."

CHAPTER TWENTY-SIX

"I MEAN TO CAUSE you absolutely no harm," June said, holding up her hands and taking a step back, almost tripping on some of the broken bricks on the floor. "I want to help you. Let me find someone who can ease your burden."

"The only person who could ease my burden is long dead," Lucy replied, stepping forward with the broken brick once again in her right hand. "All I can do now is try to finish her work, and look after the children here. The First Order have promised me that chance, just as long as I finish you off. You have to admit, they have quite the flair for the dramatic."

"Do you truly believe that killing me will end your suffering?" June asked. "Do you think it will bring your mother back?"

"I think it'll allow me to start again," Lucy explained. "The children are still here, still haunting this place after so many years. They need guidance and help, and Elspeth Barker can't offer them any of that. What they need is someone who cares for them, and I can be that person. My mother did what she had to do in 1942, she showed them great mercy, but she was denied the chance to care for them. Now, thanks to a miracle, I have been given that chance, and I won't let anyone or anything stop me."

"I remember your mother now," June replied, backing away further. "I remember her kindness, at least at first. I could tell that she was a good woman who just made one terrible mistake, and I'm sure her mind simply broke because she couldn't understand so much horror. But she was a good person deep down, and she certainly wouldn't want you to kill anyone."

"Who said anything about killing?" Lucy asked, edging closer. "Wait, I did, didn't I? Well, plans change. I'm not a murderer, Sister June, and the First Order certainly don't want you dead. Not yet, at least. They just want me to rough you up a little, and break your soul... and leave you in the same state my mother was left in when she left this place."

"Lucy, listen to me very carefully," June replied, "if -"

Before she could finish, she saw several young girls standing over by the far wall. She turned and saw more near the door, and more over in the corner; all the girls had deathly white faces and dark, haunted eyes, and June even recognized some of them from her brief stay at Holdham Hall as a child.

"You came back," Alexandra said darkly. "We didn't think you'd do that."

"You made everything so much more complicated," Judith added. "We just want to be left in peace forever. Why can't anyone understand that?"

"We don't like to be reminded of what happened to us," Wendy explained. "We can all remember the pain if we try really hard, but we don't want to do that. We want to be happy, and we want to be looked after."

"We're children," Alexandra continued. "That's what children want, they want to be cared for. We're just... children who have been children for a very long time."

"You shouldn't still be here," June told her. "You should have moved on and found peace."

"I agree," Alexandra replied, taking a step forward, "but sometimes life just isn't fair. We would have been alright, though, if you hadn't come and ruined everything. We still remember you, June. We all do. And we remember how Sister Martha looked after us. Why did you make her leave?"

"I didn't," June said, turning to Lucy again. "It wasn't my fault! I was just a child!"

"A very precocious child, by all accounts," Lucy suggested. "How could you have been so stupid? How did you not realize that all the other children were dead?"

"I'm sorry," June said, turning to Alexandra again, "I -"

In that moment, she saw that the dead girl was gone; *all* the dead children had disappeared in the blink of an eye, and when she looked around June realized that something else had changed as well. The hall seemed different, as if all the damage from the bomb had been undone. Looking up, she even saw a ceiling high above, although a few seconds later she heard the advancing whine of a falling bomb.

"No," she whispered, "I -"

Before she could finish, the bomb slammed into the ground just meters from the school. The entire building shook, and huge chunks of masonry began to crash down as the ceiling and part of the wall collapsed. Shaken off her feet, June dropped down onto her hands and knees and felt the ground shake as debris rained down all around her. The collapse seemed to last forever, until finally June was left on the ground as the clamor of the explosion was slowly replaced by the screams of dying children.

"No," she said again, looking all around, "I can't -"

As soon as she saw them, her heart broke. Some of the children were clearly dead already, partially crushed by falling chunks of stone; one girl lay nearby with part of the ceiling having smashed down onto her chest, leaving splattered blood across the ground, while another was visible only from the waist down, with her torso and head having been obliterated. Those, however, were in some ways the lucky ones; a dozen or more girls were partially trapped, with limbs and parts of their torsos smashed or ripped away by the disaster. Turning to look all around, overcome by the horror, June finally spotted Alexandra on the ground with the entire left side of her body trapped under fallen masonry.

"Help me!" Alexandra sobbed. "Somebody... it hurts so much!"

"Everything's going to be alright," June stammered.

"Is that it?" Lucy snapped. "Is that your default response to everything, Sister June? Do you have nothing to offer these poor dying girls except meaningless words? At least my mother *did* something."

"She killed them!" June protested.

"She finished them off," Lucy replied

darkly. "The war killed them."

"June?" another voice gasped. "June, help me!"

Turning, June saw Meredith on the ground nearby; or, at least, what was left of Meredith. With her body crushed by a huge chunk of stone, part of the skin on her face had been ripped away, revealing the glistening and bloodied meat below. June instinctively stepped over to help her, before stopping as she saw that more and more blood was gushing from her friend's body.

"June?" Meredith whimpered. "Why aren't you doing something, June?"

"Yes, June," Lucy continued. "Why aren't you doing something?"

"I can't," June said, her voice tense with fear. "I just... there's nothing I can do."

"Did we all hear that right?" Lucy asked. "The great and wonderful Sister June finally admits that she can't do anything to help those in need!"

"These girls have been dead for a long time," June said, kneeling next to the spectral figure of Meredith on the floor and reaching out with trembling hands. "They were dead before I ever set foot in Holdham Hall. There was never anything I could have done for them."

"But would you have done what my mother did?" Lucy asked, stepping up behind her. "Would you have had the heart to show these girls mercy and end their suffering?"

"You mean... kill them?" June replied, her eyes filling with tears as she watched Meredith's gasping breaths. "I truly don't know whether I could have done that."

"That's why my mother was a great woman," Lucy sneered, "who was cruelly punished for her devotion. Even after the girls died, she only wanted to stay and look after them, but you showed up and ruined everything. The girls have been left alone ever since, at least until now, because I'm going to continue my mother's work. And you, Sister June, are going to pay the way you should have paid all those years ago."

"No," June replied, "I -"

Before she could finish, Lucy cracked the brick down against the back of June's head, knocking her to the floor. Gasping, June reached back and felt blood trickling from a wound on her scalp; she looked up and saw Lucy towering over her, silhouetted against the starry night sky, and already she felt as if she might pass out at any moment. Wincing, she tried to get up, only to feel a cold dead hand gripping her wrist. She froze for a few seconds, not daring to look, before finally she turned and saw Meredith's bloodied and rotten face snarling at her.

"You shouldn't have come here!" Meredith screamed, lunging forward and grabbing June by the shoulders, as all the other dead girls joined in as well, grabbing a sobbing June under the mass of their swarming bodies. "You should have left us all alone!"

CHAPTER TWENTY-SEVEN

1945...

"THERE WE GO," DOCTOR Ward said, as he dabbed at the small cut on June's forehead. "Nothing a little cotton wool won't fix. Don't worry, June, you're going to be right as rain."

Sitting on the edge of a chair in the doctor's office, June stared straight ahead. Morning had come, and the doctor was being very kind to her; everyone was being kind to her, in fact, yet she still couldn't quite stop replaying the previous night's events over and over in her mind. She remembered Sister Martha screaming at her, she remembered the other girls at the school being very scary, and she remembered...

Furrowing her brow, she realized that the

details were already starting to fade, that her memories weren't sticking properly in her mind, and that Doctor Ward was talking again.

"June?" he said as she looked up at him. "Did you hear me?"

"I'm sorry," she replied, sounding increasingly dazed, "but... I don't know."

"I said that you're going to be fine to leave today," he explained, heading over to the counter and setting the bloodied cotton wool in a metal dish. "I want to have someone keep an eye on you, of course, but that's only as a precaution. You're a member of the walking wounded right now, but all the injuries are superficial." He turned and smiled at her. "Stiff upper lip, eh? That's the British way, and to be honest it's very helpful. Got me through the war."

June looked over at him, but she was still struggling to piece everything together. The events of the previous few days were slipping from her mind like stray fragments of a dream. The more she tried to remember, the more she felt as if all her thoughts were fading to become mere impressions, just snapshots of her time at Holdham Hall.

"I hear you went through quite an ordeal," Doctor Ward continued. "Something about a big old school, and being abandoned on your own for days, and a crazy nun? A couple of the police officers needed stitches, apparently they were bitten by the nun. Now there's a story to tell people, eh? Hard to believe that such things can happen, isn't it? But I suppose you're walking proof of that. What matters is that you're here now, and that you're in very safe hands."

"Where's Sister Martha?" June asked cautiously.

"I believe she's been taken away so she can be looked after," he told her. "Don't worry about that, she's gone now and you won't ever have to see her again."

"Where's Meredith?"

"Who's Meredith?"

"One of the girls at the school," June told him.

"You mean the dead girls?"

"Is Meredith dead?" She thought for a moment. "Yes, I think she is. I think I remember something about her being dead. I just don't know whether I remember her dying. It's very confusing."

"I don't think you need to worry about all of that," he continued, checking his watch. "June, some very nice ladies are going to come and collect you this afternoon, and you're actually a very lucky little girl. You're going to be so well looked after, and you'll never have to worry about anything or want anything ever again. As for Holdham Hall, I think you should put it out of your mind as much as possible."

He waited for a reply. After a moment, seeing that June still seemed dazed, he made his way back over and checked the cuts on her head one more time.

"I just want to be sure you don't have any kind of concussion," he murmured. "No, it all looks fine, I'm not too worried. June, I want you to wait right here and I'll have Connie bring you some milk and biscuits. And then, when the nice ladies come to collect you, you can start your new life. How does that sound?"

"Thank you," June said, still dazed as she looked up at him. "That sounds really nice... I think."

***

"This time I've made bloody sure that there aren't going to be any screw-ups," Mr. Holden said between drags on his cigarettes, sitting on the wall outside the front of the surgery. "Those bloody stupid -"

Spotting June as she emerged from the main door, he stepped over to her.

"There's the girl of the hour," he beamed with a big, slightly unreal smile. "How are you feeling, June? Are you all chipper and raring to go?"

"I think so," June replied.

"She's fine," Connie said, still holding

June's hand. "Doctor Ward wants her to have lots of rest and recuperation, which I don't think she'll mind too much. And he wants a doctor near the convent to take a look at her in a week or two, just to make sure that everything's alright."

"I'm sure that can be arranged," Mr. Holden said, patting June on the shoulder. "You're such a lucky young lady. You know, back in the day, the nuns from St. Jude's used to visit Holdham Hall and select one special girl to go and live with them. Obviously that all stopped a few years ago when the... unpleasantness happened, but I spoke to them on the telephone and they're willing to revive the practice just for you. How does that make you feel, June?"

"I don't know," June said cautiously. "I don't think I remember very much from the past few days. Where's Meredith?"

"Meredith?"

"Meredith's dead," June added softly, under her breath. "I remember that part, but I don't quite remember how or..."

Her voice trailed off as a car stopped nearby. Lost in thought, June barely even noticed as several sets of footsteps approached, or as Mr. Holden started speaking to a woman.

"You'll be fine," Connie told June, slipping her hand away. "I promise. Just be brave, June. You can do that, can't you?"

June looked up at her, momentarily confused, before turning to see that Mr. Holden was talking to three nuns. Blinking, June saw that the women were wearing beautiful black dresses, complete with head coverings; something about the women immediately struck June as being very comforting. In some ways they reminded her of Sister Martha, but she quickly put such thoughts from her mind as one of the nuns turned and smiled at her. In that instant, June somehow felt as if – after drifting for so long since the deaths of her parents – she had finally found the right place to be.

"She's a good kid," Mr. Holden was telling one of the nuns. "A little shaken up, but fundamentally alright. I'm sure she'll forget most of what happened to her. You know what children are like, they always muddle through things. She acts quite mature for her age, more than any girl I've ever looked after, but don't let that fool you."

"And the incident at Holdham Hall," one of the nuns replied, "is all dealt with?"

"Just a brief bureaucratic error," Mr. Holden said, rolling his eyes, "and some craziness with a mad nun." He paused for a moment. "Uh, no offense intended, obviously."

"Sister Martha was from our convent," the nun told him. "She was a good woman, but obviously at some point she went astray. We shall pray for her soul as she receives the treatment she very much needs, but I think our focus now should be on this poor young soul. Might I go and introduce myself?"

"I should be getting off," Mr. Holden muttered, heading over and patting June hard on the head before walking to his car. "Goodbye, June. Second time lucky, but I think this time I'm leaving you in very capable hands!"

Not really knowing what to say, June watched as he climbed into his car. A moment later she turned and looked up, and she swallowed hard as she saw the three nuns smiling back down at her. She opened her mouth to introduce herself, but she still felt strangely groggy and for a few seconds she could only look up at them and wonder where she was going to be taken.

"Hello, June," one of the nuns said, reaching down and gently placing a hand on her shoulder. "I'm so very glad to meet you. I've heard a lot about you, young lady, and I hope that we can become friends. Do you think you'd like that?"

June thought for a moment, before gently nodding.

"We have a short drive ahead of us," the nun continued, before holding her hand out for June to shake. "I've got a good feeling about this, June. I think we're going to get along just fine. My name is Sister Margaret, and today I'm going to take you to your new home at our lovely convent called St.

Jude's. How does that sound?"

CHAPTER TWENTY-EIGHT

1985...

"IT'S SO SAD, ISN'T it?" Stefan said, stopping next to the table in the mortuary and looking at the naked woman on the slab. "I'll never understand why some families disown the dead, just because..."

His voice trailed off for a moment.

"Well, you know," he continued, looking at the woman's face. "I've been doing this job for a long time, but there's something about suicides that always gets to me, especially when they're so young. Apparently this one threw herself into the river in Zurich. When her family were informed, they basically said that they wanted nothing to do with her, they wouldn't even arrange a funeral. Something about bringing shame to them."

For a few seconds he continued to stare at her face, before picking up a clipboard that lay on the counter.

"Eloise Tate," he read out loud. "She's being sent to the crematorium down the road, and then she'll be given a modest burial. Just something to mark her passing."

"Let's get her ready to be shipped out," Anders replied, wandering past and heading over to the door. "Sorry, it's just that I'm so busy today. I don't have time to stand around being morbid about every body we have to process."

Once Anders was out of the room, Stefan looked at the cuts on the woman's chest. The autopsy had been fairly standard and had determined – as expected – that Eloise had drowned. Having conducted thousands of autopsies over the years, Stefan had learned to not dwell on them too much, yet somehow the death of Eloise Tate was nagging at his mind. As he headed to the desk and made a few last-minute notes, he was already planning to pick up a bottle of wine on the way home and drink all his cares away.

That always worked.

Hearing a creaking sound coming from over his shoulder, he added a few more notes before signing the bottom of the sheet. He read over what he'd written, and although he heard a couple of bumps he failed to really recognize that anything might be wrong, until he turned to look at the corpse and saw that it was now suddenly standing up next to the slab.

"What?" he stammered, staring into the dead woman's eyes as she in turn stared back at her. "How..."

In that moment, part of her chest fell open again, revealing the pale organs inside. Looking down, Eloise stared at her exposed lung for a few seconds before gently trying to push the flap of skin back into place.

"You're dead," Stefan said, his voice trembling with shock, "you... I... I conducted your... you..."

He stared for a moment longer, before letting out a gasp and slumping down unconscious against the floor.

Standing naked next to the slab, with thick marks and cuts all over her body, Eloise remained completely motionless at first. She looked down at Stefan but showed no real sign of emotion, and then she spotted her own reflection in a nearby mirror. Again, she displayed no reaction other than a kind of blank calm, although her gaze lingered for a few more minutes as she looked at the stitches and other marks criss-crossing her chest. A moment later the flap began to open again, marking the spot where she'd been opened up for her autopsy. Eloise reached up and tried to hold her body together, and then she turned and saw some wire and a needle resting nearby on one of the benches.

***

By the time she'd found some spare clothes in the storage room, along with a hat that she could use to cover the thick scar running entirely around the top of her head, Eloise was finally getting used to her body again. Sure, the joints were stiff and she could tell that her organs were very much in the wrong place, but she didn't really need her heart or her lungs anymore.

Opening the back door, she stepped out into the cold afternoon air and tried to work out why everything felt so still. After a few more seconds she realized the unfortunate and slightly disturbing truth: she wasn't breathing, she could even fake any breaths, and besides her bloodless body was feeling increasingly cold. In fact, she was no longer entirely sure that she was going to be able to stay mobile, and she worried that the autopsy might have caused far too much damage to her limbs.

More than anything, as she looked down at her hands, she realized that her mind and body now felt so very separate, as if her physical form was now little more than a spluttering engine made of flesh and bone. A mild sense of nausea permeated her gut, but otherwise she felt increasingly cold and blank, and she realized that she could barely even keep hold of her thoughts, although one question was going round and round in her mind as if demanding to be answered.

Why am I doing this?

"I'm dead," she whispered, remembering the moment when she'd plunged into the cold river. "I died. I should... I should be resting. I should be asleep. I should be... gone..."

Her mind was rushing with thoughts, but she kept thinking back to her last night in Zurich. She'd been wandering the darkened streets for hours, and eventually she'd bumped into a strange and rather enigmatic man who'd made a few cryptic comments. At the time she'd been unable to put her finger on her concerns, to work out exactly why she found the man so strange, but now she realized that he'd seemed barely human; sure, he'd looked like a man, but she couldn't shake the feeling that something else had been hiding behind his human face and his human eyes, something perhaps part human but also part...

Something else.

Something dangerous.

"I'm dead," she said again, trying to shock herself to her senses with those words. "I shouldn't be here, this is all wrong, it's unnatural, I..."

She felt as if she should be crying, yet no tears reached her eyes. She tried to take a deep breath, only to find that she was unable to do so. Finally, trying not to panic, she began to stumble away from the back of the building, crossing the empty parking lot and hugging herself in a vain attempt to generate a little warmth. She almost tripped a couple of times, and weakness dogged every step as she felt as if she might be about to collapse. Finally, reaching the far end of the lot, she reached out and steadied herself for a few seconds against the barrier, and in that moment she realized that she had no idea where she was going.

Since waking up on the slab, she'd been filled with a determined need to get away. Now that she was out of the mortuary, however, she looked around and realized that no particular direction seemed any better than the rest. She tried to swallow, but this time she was unable even to do that; her body was just about functioning, but every action felt so strange and unnatural, and she was barely able to do anything other than move herself around.

Seconds later, hearing footsteps, she turned to see a man making his way toward her. She opened her mouth to call out to him, but at the last moment she realized that she'd seen him before. This was the same man she'd met in Zurich during that last, fateful night.

"My name's John," she remembered him explaining. "I'm just in town for a short visit. I have a few... jobs that I need to get done."

"What are you doing here?" she gasped.

"I'm sorry I couldn't get to you sooner," he replied, stopping on the other side of the barrier and looking her up and down. "Scheduling has never been my strong point, and certain matters in England required my attendance. As, indeed, they will do again shortly. Would you mind if I fill you in on a few things in the car?" He nodded toward a black limousine, parked over on the other side of the street. "There really isn't much time."

"Who are you?" she asked.

"I haven't been honest with you, Eloise," he continued. "From the moment I first saw you in Zurich, long before we properly met, I've known that you're perfect for a little task that I have in mind."

"I'm dead," she told him. "I... I think I am, anyway."

She held her hands up.

"I'm not breathing. My heart's not beating. I've been cut up, and I think I even had an autopsy."

"All of those things are absolutely true," he replied, before reaching a hand out toward her. "I need you to come with me now, Eloise, and I'm afraid that I can't offer you any uplifting words. You're going to have to do something for me, and it's going to be horrible and painful and slow. There's no benefit for you whatsoever. You're going to hate every excruciating second, but I'm truly sorry. There's simply no other way."

Leaning forward slightly, he took hold of her hand.

"My, you really *are* cold, aren't you?" he added. "We must go now. A friend of mine is in great need of your help."

CHAPTER TWENTY-NINE

TWENTY-FOUR HOURS LATER, SISTER Lucy stood on the gravel driveway outside Holdham Hall and watched as a figure was carried out on a stretcher. She saw Sister June's face, with wide-open eyes staring up at the gray sky, and she couldn't help but allow herself a faint smile.

"You know," she said after a moment, as June was loaded into the back of an ambulance, "part of me still wishes you'd let me kill her. It would have been so easy, and I would have enjoyed it so very much."

"That wasn't the plan," a voice replied. "You did exactly what we asked. You broke her mind. Now the rest of the procedure will be conducted at Shadborne."

Turning, Lucy saw that Cardinal Abruzzo

was making his way over from a nearby parked car.

"What exactly are you going to do with her?" she asked.

"That's confidential," he explained, "but let's just say that I flew in from Italy especially for this particular task. There are people at the very top of the First Order who want Sister June to suffer, while I am primarily focused on the task of scraping her brain for any last residual drop of information. Happily, those two needs can be met in a manner that is highly efficient."

"Shadborne's a hospital, isn't it?"

"Of sorts."

"You're not going to make her *better*, are you?"

"No," he replied, "we're definitely not going to do that. Let's just say that Sister June has irritated the wrong people. We're not usually so strict when it comes to retiring First Order agents, but dear Sister June is to be subjected to some very cruel and unusual punishment. It's not exactly my idea, but I'm happy to go along with it."

"Make her suffer a little extra, just for me," Lucy said, watching as the doors at the rear of the ambulance were slammed shut. "Meanwhile, I am going to stay here at Holdham Hall and continue the work my mother started. The ghosts of those children are still here, and they need to be looked after. I shall care for them and tend to their needs, and show them as much kindness as I can manage." She hesitated, close to tears, and then she stepped forward and surprised Cardinal Abruzzo by giving him a big hug. "Thank you so much," she sobbed. "You have no idea how much this means to me."

"Quite," he replied awkwardly. "The ambulance is ready. I have to go."

"Of course," she replied, turning and looking with great anticipation toward Holdham Hall. "My entire life has been building up to this moment!" she gasped, placing her hands together in prayer. "I hope my mother can see me! I hope she's proud! I hope I can stay here for a very long time."

"Why not stay here forever?" Cardinal Abruzzo asked, before raising a pistol and shooting her in the back of the head, then watching as her lifeless body crumpled to the ground. "Don't worry," he added, "I'll get somebody to drag your corpse inside. Then you can be with those ghostly little girls forever."

***

A few minutes later, as the ambulance sped along the road leading away from Holdham Hall, Sarah Cole leaned over Sister June and peered into her eyes.

"She's not responding," she pointed out to her fellow paramedic. "She's barely even blinking."

"Apparently she saw something in that house that broke her mind," Tom Walter replied, as he slid a needle into June's arm and gave her an injection. "I've heard about that sort of thing before, but I've never actually seen it. Sometimes the human mind just witnesses something that it can't comprehend, something too terrible, and it simply breaks."

"And the guy who went in the car that sped off ahead of us," Sarah continued, "was some kind of... priest?"

"I think it's best to not ask too many questions," Tom told her. "We're being paid very well for a few hours' work, and I for one am happy to do what they asked. They use shell companies wrapped in shell companies to employ us, and I figure anyone who wants that much secrecy is welcome to it."

"But doesn't it feel a little odd?" she asked. "Who are these people who hired us, and what do they want with a nun who seems to have a terrible case of PTSD?"

"I don't know," Tom said, sounding as if his patience was starting to wear thin, "and I don't care. Seriously, Sarah, stop worrying and -"

Suddenly something slammed against the ambulance's roof. They both looked up and saw a heavy dent, and a moment later the entire vehicle swerved off the road.

"Hold on!" Tom shouted. "I think we're about to -"

Before he could finish, the ambulance struck the side of a tree stump and flipped, crashing down onto its side with such force that it immediately began to roll. Sarah and Tom tried desperately to hold onto something, but they were thrown around as Sister June – still strapped to the stretcher – slammed against the roof and then tipped onto her side. For the next few seconds the ambulance simply continued to roll, mixing everything up inside until finally the vehicle came to a crashing rest on its side.

"Are you okay?" Tom gasped, struggling to haul himself up. "Sarah, are you hurt?"

Scrambling toward her, he reached out and tilted her head so that he could see her face, only to flinch as soon as he spotted the thick bloodied wound on her forehead. Her eyes were wide open, but when he checked for a pulse he found nothing. Clambering over Sister June's overturned stretcher, he began to administer the kiss of life to Sarah, desperately trying to save her even though deep down he knew that she'd been killed in the crash. He worked frantically for a few seconds, until something slammed hard against the ambulance's dented rear doors.

"Who's there?" Tom shouted, pulling back as the thing – whatever it might be – hit the doors again. "What do you want?"

He waited, now he heard a faint growling sound coming from outside. His first thought was that somehow the ambulance had been attacked by wolves, or by angry dogs, but a moment later one of the doors fell away and he saw something even more terrifying.

"A bear?" he stammered. "What... I mean... how? I mean..."

His voice trailed off, and a moment later the bear let out an almighty roar that made the entire overturned ambulance shudder. Pulling back further toward the other end of the vehicle, Tom clambered directly over Sarah's body, barely even noticing this time as his left foot kicked her in the face; horrified by the sight of the bear, all Tom could think about was the need to get away, and a moment later he climbed through into the driver's section of the ambulance, where he froze for a fraction of a second as he saw that a large branch had crashed through the windshield, impaling the driver through the face and poking out through the rear of the seat.

Behind him, the bear roared again. Turning, Tom watched as the animal smashed the other rear door open and began to climb onboard. The patient's stretcher was on its side, wedged against the wall, but Tom had lost all interest in trying to help the woman; instead, he climbed over the dead driver, trying to ignore the sticky blood as he pushed the door open and threw himself out. Landing hard on the ground, he immediately hauled himself up and turned to look at the ambulance again, just as the vehicle began to shake. The bear roared for a third time, accompanied by the sound of equipment smashing inside, and Tom stepped back until he tripped on a branch. Falling to the ground, he quickly scrambled to his feet before turning and racing away as fast as he could manage, hurrying across the grass and then up onto the tarmac.

"Help!" he stammered, not daring to shout too loudly as he ran along the road. "Somebody help me! There's a bear! There's -"

Finally stopping and looking back, he saw to his immense relief that at least the bear wasn't following. The ambulance was shaking, and Tom could only assume that the bear – which he figured must be rabid and insane – had started eating the dead bodies in the back. A moment later the radio attached to his waist flickered to life, and Tom pulled it up as he kept his eyes fixed firmly on the ambulance.

"Is everything okay with you guys?" a voice asked over the radio. "Our tracker shows you've stopped moving."

"Bear," Tom stammered, his voice tense with abject terror. "We got attacked. There's a.. a... we got attacked by a bear!"

CHAPTER THIRTY

"MOVE!" A VOICE SHOUTED, as several armed men stepped out of the limousine with their guns already raised. "Secure the patient at all costs!"

Ahead, the ambulance lay on its side, in the same spot where it had crashed off the road earlier. Stepping out from the limousine, Cardinal Abruzzo looked over at the vehicle for a moment, before hearing a gunshot nearby. He looked over his shoulder just in time to see Tom slump to the ground with a fresh bullet lodged in his head, while the fourth armed guard stepped over the corpse and made his way over to join the others.

"You know the deal," Abruzzo told the man, adjusting his collar a little. "The patient in that ambulance is a category one asset for the First Order, which means -"

Before he could finish, a loud roar rang out and the ambulance shuddered again. With their guns still raised, the armed men began to make their way toward the edge of the road, and a moment later they watched as the bear lumbered into view, dragging the patient still attached to the stretcher.

"Don't harm the nun!" Abruzzo yelled. "Just get her away from that damn thing!"

Spotting the guns, the bear paused for a moment before slowly lowering the stretcher to the ground. Stepping over the patient, the bear began to make its way up the grass verge, finally stepping onto the road.

"Fire!" Abruzzo screamed.

The four men did as they were told, immediately shooting at the bear. Their bullets slammed into the creature's body, causing it to let out a cry of pain as it pulled back; at the same time, its roar became louder still, almost shaking the tarmac.

"It's not dropping!" one of the men yelled. "We've hit it a dozen times already, why isn't it down?"

"There is a slight possibility," Abruzzo warned him, "that this creature is capable of... regenerating any wounds."

"Are you serious?" the man snapped, turning to him. "You didn't think to mention this sooner?"

"Try one of these," Abruzzo replied, reaching into his pocket and taking out a small box, then stepping over to the man and opening the box to reveal a set of six silver bullets. "You might find that these things cause wounds that... take a little longer to heal."

Grabbing a handful of the bullets, the man quickly reloaded his gun. This time he took a moment to aim more carefully; the bear, although clearly irritated by the shots so far, was already starting to advance toward the men.

"Such a magnificent beast," Abruzzo murmured, staring with a sense of genuine wonder at the creature. "So much power. So much fury. So much potential. Such a shame that it's all harnessed for such a wretched cause."

As soon as the man next to him fired, hitting the bear with one of the silver bullets, an anguished cry ran out from the animal. Turning and lumbering away, the bear seemed almost to be limping now; the first silver bullet was embedded in its flank, and the man adjusted his aim for a moment before firing again and again, hitting the bear's back and bringing forth even louder cries.

"Grab the stretcher!" Abruzzo yelled. "Get her off it and bring her to the car!"

Two of the men hurried over to the stretcher. Pulling the straps free, they found that one of the buckles was caught on the nun's habit. The bear was already showing signs of recovery, turning to roar at the men, but at the moment the sixth and final silver bullet burst through its throat, sending it crashing back down against the tarmac.

"Hurry!" Abruzzo shouted. "Those things won't last forever, and I'm not *made* of silver bullets!"

Stepping aside, he watched as the men loaded the nun into the back of the limousine. Already the bear was showing signs of recovery, although it was clearly still in pain and its back legs seemed not to be working properly. Abruzzo watched for a moment, still mesmerized by the sight, before one of the armed men pulled him over to the vehicle and forced him inside. The other men shot a few more times at the bear with their ordinary bullets, before climbing into the limousine just as the driver pushed his foot down against the throttle pedal.

"Sir, are you okay?" one of the men asked, as his colleagues set the patient down against the limousine's floor.

"I am now," Abruzzo replied, looking out the rear window and watching as the bear and the overturned ambulance receded into the distance. "I can assure you, however, that the consequence if we'd failed today would have been extremely unfortunate. For all of us."

***

Bone twisted against muscle, splitting and cracking open, constantly mending and breaking again in an orgy of mangled matter. Occasionally fresh muscles emerged from the mess, complete with veins that throbbed and in some cases burst; blood dribbled down the sides and was quickly absorbed back into the endlessly turning carcass that for several minutes lay in the middle of the road, accompanied by a series of dark, guttural groans that gradually began to sound a little more human.

Finally, slowly, a human arm emerged from the mess of tendons and muscle and bone, ripping its way forward until a hand tried to grip the tarmac. Skin was already growing across the hand, and a moment later the flesh a little further toward the elbow briefly became swollen, popping out a silver bullet before sinking back once more to a vaguely human shape. Next came the shoulders, huge and powerful, before a neck rose up followed by a head. For the next few seconds all the basic ingredients of a human face were in place, albeit mixed around in a soupy mess until they began to reassemble themselves in a more familiar pattern, with patches of hair growing in a matter of seconds.

Once the legs were formed, the figure started to raise himself up. Most of the body was coming together in its proper form now, but in a few spots there were mistakes that had to be rectified; the figure briefly began to grow a third leg, before the knotted mass of muscle was reabsorbed into the central core, and a bulb of half a dozen kneecaps briefly tried to support the left leg before this too was rearranged. Finally, slowly, the figure let out a growl of pain as he stood up straight; naked now and with a few traces of smeared blood, he felt the last of the bullets falling out from his muscles and landing on the ground next to his bare feet.

Tilting his head to the right, John grimaced as he stretched to sort out one last knot of nerves that had misaligned just below his jaw. And then, after tilting his head briefly in the other direction, he was finished.

"That," he murmured darkly, staring at the empty road ahead, "was not fun."

The transformation had taken longer than usual, since the silver bullets had still been polluting his body. Popping the bullets out had required tremendous effort, such that a change that would usually only take a couple of minutes had in fact taken almost ten. He could still feel the screaming pain of each bullet entering his body, so much worse that the mere irritation of the ordinary bullets that he'd been able to more or less ignore. Looking down, he saw the silver bullets on the ground and was unable to resist briefly contorting his face into a rictus of anger and disgust.

"Humans," he grimaced. "Always coming up with new ways to piss me off."

Looking back over at the ambulance, he saw what remained of the driver in the front, his face still smashed by the branch that had burst through the windshield. There was no coming back for that guy, he reasoned with a dismissive sneer, and as he began to make his way back toward the rear of the wrecked vehicle he barely even noticed his bare feet treading on pieces of shattered glass. Stopping to look at the ambulance's bent and twisted rear doors, he stared for a moment before looking up; for a moment his senses tingled as he picked up the faintest buzz of something high in the sky, something with potential to watch his every move. He looked at the back of the ambulance again, fully aware that he was possibly being observed, and then – as he felt the anger bursting through his body – he picked up a chunk of twisted metal and threw it against the vehicle's side, puncturing a large hole.

"I'll find you, Sister June," he snarled, clenching both fists. "I don't know how long it'll take, but I'll get to Shadborne somehow and I swear I'll find you. And then I'll either save you, or if they've done too much to you already... I'll put you out of your misery."

EPILOGUE

TWO WEEKS LATER, CARDINAL Abruzzo walked up the steps leading into the First Order's main chapel complex. He'd passed this way many times over the years, but this time he did something completely new. As he reached the top of the steps, instead of reaching out to automatically open the door, he hesitated for a few seconds.

Somewhere in the distance, bells rang out over the late-night Roman skyline.

"Don't worry," he remembered Doctor Guinness saying a short while earlier, as they'd both been standing in an office at Shadborne, "we'll take good care of her. *Really* good care."

"What exactly has Sister Josephine asked you to do?" Abruzzo had replied.

"Hasn't she told you?"

"It's not technically part of my remit," he'd admitted, "so... not exactly."

"She wants us to scoop out all her memories," Guinness had explained, "and make sure we get everything. By the end, there'll be nothing left of her except an empty shell, and usually at that point we'd terminate the flesh. In this case, however, Sister Josephine has asked us to keep her alive for as long as possible."

"Why?"

"She says that while there's even the slightest chance of Sister June feeling pain, she wants that prolonged for as long as possible. I told her there'll be no real way to determine whether there's much brain activity, but I don't think she cares too much about that. I think for Sister Josephine it's personal, and she's happy just knowing there's a chance that Sister June's existing in everlasting agony."

Now, standing in front of the door, Cardinal Abruzzo couldn't help but whisper a silent prayer. He'd done a lot for Sister Josephine over the years, and there had been plenty of times when he'd been forced to question the morality of his own actions; he'd told himself that he was working to serve the greater good, that the First Order's mission was more important than anything else, yet this time he couldn't escape a niggling fear that some invisible line had been crossed. If Sister June had really reached the end of her usefulness, why couldn't she be allowed to rest in peace? Why should she be tortured, potentially for years and years, just to satisfy Sister Josephine's bloodlust?

"Forgive us," he whispered now. "I only hope that what we're doing now is acceptable as part of the bigger picture. That the ends will justify the means."

He took a deep breath, and then he opened the door and stepped inside the chapel complex.

***

"You accelerated the process?" Abruzzo said a short while later, standing on the viewing gallery and staring with a sense of incredulity at the reconstructed arch below. "I thought I explained that -"

"I don't have time to wait!" Sister Josephine hissed, sitting next to him in her wheelchair and smiling as she watched the technicians attaching another fragment to the gate. "I spoke to the team and they promised me they could work ten times faster if they just abandoned a few of your silly little protocols."

"Those protocols are in place for a very good reason," Abruzzo warned her. "If we rush this project -"

"If we rush this project," she replied,

interrupting him yet again, "then we'll get it finished faster." She looked up at him with a faint smile. "That is, assuming you trust the team you've assembled for this task. I provided you with a full budget so that you could bring in the very best people from around the world. You didn't fail in that task, did you?"

"Of course not," he replied through gritted teeth.

"I could have asked Cardinal Boone to oversee this most crucial of projects," she reminded him, "but I opted for you because of your vim and vigor. I still have faith in you, but that faith will not last forever. I'm old, and I need results soon. You must understand that."

"I do," he said, looking at the technicians again, as they all gathered on one side of the arch. "I just know how important this is, and I also know that if we fail we might not get another chance for centuries."

"Then we must not fail," she purred.

Abruzzo watched as the technicians continued their work, and after a few seconds he realized that they seemed a little agitated about something. He told himself not to worry, but he'd seen them working before and he knew it was unusual for all of them to be attending to one supposedly simple task. Finally, just as he was trying to stay calm, the lead technician from the group broke away from the rest and began to make his way up to the viewing gallery.

"What's going on?" Sister Josephine asked. "Is something wrong?"

"I'm sure it's all fine," Abruzzo said tensely, as Doctor Nakano approached. "I'm sure they just want to double-check something with us, that's all."

"We've got a problem," Nakano said, stopping in front of them. "We've been using the new scanner to catalog all the pieces and -"

"Get to the point," Sister Josephine replied, cutting him off. "Don't sugarcoat things for me. If there's an issue, I want to know as quickly as possible so that we can get it fixed."

"We're missing a piece."

"Impossible!" she snapped angrily. "We used state-of-the-art equipment to bring everything from that underground site!"

"I know," Nakano replied, "I supervised all of that myself. Yet somehow we're missing a small piece of the gate, and as I'm sure you know, we need all of it. If even the tiniest crumb is missing, it simply won't function."

"How can we be missing anything?" Sister Josephine asked, clearly filled with panic as she looked up at Abruzzo. "We've been so careful! How could even the smallest speck of an atom have escaped from that site?"

"I don't know," Abruzzo told her, "but we

can find out. We'll leave no stone unturned until we're sure."

"Find it!" Sister Josephine screamed, no longer able to contain her fury. She tried to get to her feet, only to slump back into her wheelchair. "Do you hear me? I don't care where you have to go, I don't care how far you have to travel! Find that missing piece!"

***

Voices called out in the distance, in a language that she didn't entirely understand, as Stella Weaver stood looking down at the papers on her desk. Just one week into her new project at a remote Greek site, she was struggling a little with the complexities of keeping so many different stakeholders happy.

"What would you have done, Dad?" she murmured, glancing at a framed photo of her father. "You were always so completely on top of these things."

"Stella?" a voice called out, and she turned to see Mike Franklin stepping into the tent. "You'd better get out here," he continued. "A man from the ministry has turned up, and he's threatening to withdraw all our permits unless we agree to help his son set up his own museum."

"Seriously?" she replied.

"Seriously."

"Stall him," she said with a heavy sigh. "I'm on my way."

As Mike hurried back to the site, Stella reached into her pocket and pulling out a small piece of stone. She'd been carrying this particular object around as a kind of good luck talisman, even though she didn't really believe in luck at all.

"Stella," she remembered Sister June saying at the hospital back in Africa, "there's this one thing I'd like you to have." With that, she'd handed Stella a small piece of stone marked with strange lettering. "It must have got caught in my things on the way up, I'm not entirely sure how I ended up with it, but I just thought you might like to keep it as a kind of reminder of what you discovered down there. Even if you don't do anything with it on a professional level, you can always remember that you and your father discovered something truly astonishing."

"A reminder of what's possible," Stella murmured now, turning the piece of stone over in her hands for a moment, thinking back to the remarkable sights beneath the Saharan desert. "Thank you, Sister June. Wherever you are now, I hope you're having fun. As much fun as a nun *can* have, at least."

***

"Here we go," Todd said, stepping into the darkened

chamber and approaching the figure sitting strapped into a wooden chair. "Some water. Are you thirsty?"

He held the water out, but the woman – wearing nothing but a tattered white night-shirt – offered no response. After a moment Todd nudged the cup against her lips, but she still said nothing.

"You're not dead, are you?" he muttered, grabbing her hair and pulling her head back until he could see her wide-open, horrified eyes. "No, you're not dead," he chuckled as he saw the signs of sheer madness etched across her features. "You're obviously not too well, though. You're looking pale and a little thin, like maybe you've been through the wars a bit. Then again, if you were well, you probably wouldn't be here at all. This place isn't exactly famous for its therapeutic qualities."

He looked at her face for a moment longer, noticing various cuts and scars, before letting go of her hair. Her head tipped forward again, and after a few seconds some specks of drool began to dribble from her lips.

"Looks like we'll have to force food and water into you," Todd said, not sounding particularly troubled as he turned and headed to the door. Once he was outside the cell, he looked back at the new arrival. "Don't worry, Sister June," he continued, "we've got all the time in the world to get to know one another. Whatever might have happened to you in the past, none of it's important now. All we care about here is that we keep you alive while Doctor Guinness pokes around inside that head of yours. I'll be back with the feeding tube later. It's not a particularly pleasant experience, from what I can tell, but you'll just have to put up with it."

Slamming the door shut, he slid the bolt across before opening the small viewing hatch and peering into the cell. For a moment he stared at the figure slumped in the chair, and a smile slowly grew across his face.

"You'll soon get used to things here, Sister June," he added. "They all do, eventually. Oh, and welcome to Shadborne!"

NEXT IN THIS SERIES

THE SEVENTH CELL
(THE CHRONICLES OF SISTER JUNE BOOK 7)

The year is 1991. Gretchen Holdrake has been working as a cleaner at Shadborne Psychiatric Hospital for almost a decade. Everyone knows about the mysterious nun who's kept secluded in one of the wards, but only a few doctors are ever allowed into that part of the building

On one fateful day, Gretchen is called into the hospital's top secret seventh cell, where she finally meets Sister June. Or, rather, what's left of Sister June. As the horrifying truth starts to emerge, Gretchen finds herself drawn into a bizarre set of games that seem designed to destroy the incarcerated woman forever.

And then, at the edge of the hospital's grounds, Gretchen encounters a bear.

Coming soon...

Also by Amy Cross

1689
(The Haunting of Hadlow House book 1)

All Richard Hadlow wants is a happy family and a peaceful home. Having built the perfect house deep in the Kent countryside, now all he needs is a wife. He's about to discover, however, that even the most perfectly-laid plans can go horribly and tragically wrong.

The year is 1689 and England is in the grip of turmoil. A pretender is trying to take the throne, but Richard has no interest in the affairs of his country. He only cares about finding the perfect wife and giving her a perfect life. But someone – or something – at his newly-built house has other ideas. Is Richard's new life about to be destroyed forever?

Hadlow House is brand new, but already there are strange whispers in the corridors and unexplained noises at night. Has Richard been unlucky, is his new wife simply imagining things, or is a dark secret from the past about to rise up and deliver Richard's worst nightmare? Who wins when the past and the present collide?

Also by Amy Cross

The Haunting of Nelson Street
(The Ghosts of Crowford book 1)

Crowford, a sleepy coastal town in the south of England, might seem like an oasis of calm and tranquility. Beneath the surface, however, dark secrets are waiting to claim fresh victims, and ghostly figures plot revenge.

Having finally decided to leave the hustle of London, Daisy and Richard Johnson buy two houses on Nelson Street, a picturesque street in the center of Crowford. One house is perfect and ready to move into, while the other is a fire-ravaged wreck that needs a lot of work. They figure they have plenty of time to work on the damaged house while Daisy recovers from a traumatic event.

Soon, they discover that the two houses share a common link to the past. Something awful once happened on Nelson Street, something that shook the town to its core.

Also by Amy Cross

The Revenge of the Mercy Belle
(The Ghosts of Crowford book 2)

The year is 1950, and a great tragedy has struck the town of Crowford. Three local men have been killed in a storm, after their fishing boat the Mercy Belle sank. A mysterious fourth man, however, was rescue. Nobody knows who he is, or what he was doing on the Mercy Belle... and the man has lost his memory.

Five years later, messages from the dead warn of impending doom for Crowford. The ghosts of the Mercy Belle's crew demand revenge, and the whole town is being punished. The fourth man still has no memory of his previous existence, but he's married now and living under the named Edward Smith. As Crowford's suffering continues, the locals begin to turn against him.

What really happened on the night the Mercy Belle sank? Did the fourth man cause the tragedy? And will Crowford survive if this man is not sent to meet his fate?

Also by Amy Cross

The Devil, the Witch and the Whore
(The Deal book 1)

"Leave the forest alone. Whatever's out there, just let it be. Don't make it angry."

When a horrific discovery is made at the edge of town, Sheriff James Kopperud realizes the answers he seeks might be waiting beyond in the vast forest. But everybody in the town of Deal knows that there's something out there in the forest, something that should never be disturbed. A deal was made long ago, a deal that was supposed to keep the town safe. And if he insists on investigating the murder of a local girl, James is going to have to break that deal and head out into the wilderness.

Meanwhile, James has no idea that his estranged daughter Ramsey has returned to town. Ramsey is running from something, and she thinks she can find safety in the vast tunnel system that runs beneath the forest. Before long, however, Ramsey finds herself coming face to face with creatures that hide in the shadows. One of these creatures is known as the devil, and another is known as the witch. They're both waiting for the whore to arrive, but for very different reasons. And soon Ramsey is offered a terrible deal, one that could save or destroy the entire town, and maybe even the world.

Also by Amy Cross

The Soul Auction

"I saw a woman on the beach. I watched her face a demon."

Thirty years after her mother's death, Alice Ashcroft is drawn back to the coastal English town of Curridge. Somebody in Curridge has been reviewing Alice's novels online, and in those reviews there have been tantalizing hints at a hidden truth. A truth that seems to be linked to her dead mother.

"Thirty years ago, there was a soul auction."

Once she reaches Curridge, Alice finds strange things happening all around her. Something attacks her car. A figure watches her on the beach at night. And when she tries to find the person who has been reviewing her books, she makes a horrific discovery.

What really happened to Alice's mother thirty years ago? Who was she talking to, just moments before dropping dead on the beach? What caused a huge rockfall that nearly tore a nearby cliff-face in half? And what sinister presence is lurking in the grounds of the local church?

Also by Amy Cross

Darper Danver: The Complete First Series

Five years ago, three friends went to a remote cabin in the woods and tried to contact the spirit of a long-dead soldier. They thought they could control whatever happened next. They were wrong...

Newly released from prison, Cassie Briggs returns to Fort Powell, determined to get her life back on track. Soon, however, she begins to suspect that an ancient evil still lurks in the nearby cabin. Was the mysterious Darper Danver really destroyed all those years ago, or does her spirit still linger, waiting for a chance to return?

As Cassie and her ex-boyfriend Fisher are finally forced to face the truth about what happened in the cabin, they realize that Darper isn't ready to let go of their lives just yet. Meanwhile, a vengeful woman plots revenge for her brother's murder, and a New York ghost writer arrives in town to uncover the truth. Before long, strange carvings begin to appear around town and blood starts to flow once again.

Also by Amy Cross

The Ghost of Molly Holt

"Molly Holt is dead. There's nothing to fear in this house."

When three teenagers set out to explore an abandoned house in the middle of a forest, they think they've found the location where the infamous Molly Holt video was filmed.

They've found much more than that...

Tim doesn't believe in ghosts, but he has a crush on a girl who does. That's why he ends up taking her out to the house, and it's also why he lets her take his only flashlight. But as they explore the house together, Tim and Becky start to realize that something else might be lurking in the shadows.

Something that, ten years ago, suffered unimaginable pain.

Something that won't rest until a terrible wrong has been put right.

Also by Amy Cross

American Coven

He kidnapped three women and held them in his basement. He thought they couldn't fight back. He was wrong...

Snatched from the street near her home, Holly Carter is taken to a rural house and thrown down into a stone basement. She meets two other women who have also been kidnapped, and soon Holly learns about the horrific rituals that take place in the house. Eventually, she's called upstairs to take her place in the ice bath.

As her nightmare continues, however, Holly learns about a mysterious power that exists in the basement, and which the three women might be able to harness. When they finally manage to get through the metal door, however, the women have no idea that their fight for freedom is going to stretch out for more than a decade, or that it will culminate in a final, devastating demonstration of their new-found powers.

Also by Amy Cross

The Ash House

Why would anyone ever return to a haunted house?

For Diane Mercer the answer is simple. She's dying of cancer, and she wants to know once and for all whether ghosts are real.

Heading home with her young son, Diane is determined to find out whether the stories are real. After all, everyone else claimed to see and hear strange things in the house over the years. Everyone except Diane had some kind of experience in the house, or in the little ash house in the yard.

As Diane explores the house where she grew up, however, her son is exploring the yard and the forest. And while his mother might be struggling to come to terms with her own impending death, Daniel Mercer is puzzled by fleeting appearances of a strange little girl who seems drawn to the ash house, and by strange, rasping coughs that he keeps hearing at night.

The Ash House is a horror novel about a woman who desperately wants to know what will happen to her when she dies, and about a boy who uncovers the shocking truth about a young girl's murder.

AMY CROSS

Also by Amy Cross

The Curse of Wetherley House

"If you walk through that door, Evil Mary will get you."

When she agrees to visit a supposedly haunted house with an old friend, Rosie assumes she'll encounter nothing more scary than a few creaks and bumps in the night. Even the legend of Evil Mary doesn't put her off. After all, she knows ghosts aren't real. But when Mary makes her first appearance, Rosie realizes she might already be trapped.

For more than a century, Wetherley House has been cursed. A horrific encounter on a remote road in the late 1800's has already caused a chain of misery and pain for all those who live at the house. Wetherley House was abandoned long ago, after a terrible discovery in the basement, something has remained undetected within its room. And even the local children know that Evil Mary waits in the house for anyone foolish enough to walk through the front door.

Before long, Rosie realizes that her entire life has been defined by the spirit of a woman who died in agony. Can she become the first person to escape Evil Mary, or will she fall victim to the same fate as the house's other occupants?

AMY CROSS

AMY CROSS

BOOKS BY AMY CROSS

1. Dark Season: The Complete First Series (2011)
2. Werewolves of Soho (Lupine Howl book 1) (2012)
3. Werewolves of the Other London (Lupine Howl book 2) (2012)
4. Ghosts: The Complete Series (2012)
5. Dark Season: The Complete Second Series (2012)
6. The Children of Black Annis (Lupine Howl book 3) (2012)
7. Destiny of the Last Wolf (Lupine Howl book 4) (2012)
8. Asylum (The Asylum Trilogy book 1) (2012)
9. Dark Season: The Complete Third Series (2013)
10. Devil's Briar (2013)
11. Broken Blue (The Broken Trilogy book 1) (2013)
12. The Night Girl (2013)
13. Days 1 to 4 (Mass Extinction Event book 1) (2013)
14. Days 5 to 8 (Mass Extinction Event book 2) (2013)
15. The Library (The Library Chronicles book 1) (2013)
16. American Coven (2013)
17. Werewolves of Sangreth (Lupine Howl book 5) (2013)
18. Broken White (The Broken Trilogy book 2) (2013)
19. Grave Girl (Grave Girl book 1) (2013)
20. Other People's Bodies (2013)
21. The Shades (2013)
22. The Vampire's Grave and Other Stories (2013)
23. Darper Danver: The Complete First Series (2013)
24. The Hollow Church (2013)
25. The Dead and the Dying (2013)
26. Days 9 to 16 (Mass Extinction Event book 3) (2013)
27. The Girl Who Never Came Back (2013)
28. Ward Z (The Ward Z Series book 1) (2013)
29. Journey to the Library (The Library Chronicles book 2) (2014)
30. The Vampires of Tor Cliff Asylum (2014)
31. The Family Man (2014)
32. The Devil's Blade (2014)
33. The Immortal Wolf (Lupine Howl book 6) (2014)
34. The Dying Streets (Detective Laura Foster book 1) (2014)
35. The Stars My Home (2014)
36. The Ghost in the Rain and Other Stories (2014)
37. Ghosts of the River Thames (The Robinson Chronicles book 1) (2014)
38. The Wolves of Cur'eath (2014)
39. Days 46 to 53 (Mass Extinction Event book 4) (2014)
40. The Man Who Saw the Face of the World (2014)
41. The Art of Dying (Detective Laura Foster book 2) (2014)
42. Raven Revivals (Grave Girl book 2) (2014)

43. Arrival on Thaxos (Dead Souls book 1) (2014)
44. Birthright (Dead Souls book 2) (2014)
45. A Man of Ghosts (Dead Souls book 3) (2014)
46. The Haunting of Hardstone Jail (2014)
47. A Very Respectable Woman (2015)
48. Better the Devil (2015)
49. The Haunting of Marshall Heights (2015)
50. Terror at Camp Everbee (The Ward Z Series book 2) (2015)
51. Guided by Evil (Dead Souls book 4) (2015)
52. Child of a Bloodied Hand (Dead Souls book 5) (2015)
53. Promises of the Dead (Dead Souls book 6) (2015)
54. Days 54 to 61 (Mass Extinction Event book 5) (2015)
55. Angels in the Machine (The Robinson Chronicles book 2) (2015)
56. The Curse of Ah-Qal's Tomb (2015)
57. Broken Red (The Broken Trilogy book 3) (2015)
58. The Farm (2015)
59. Fallen Heroes (Detective Laura Foster book 3) (2015)
60. The Haunting of Emily Stone (2015)
61. Cursed Across Time (Dead Souls book 7) (2015)
62. Destiny of the Dead (Dead Souls book 8) (2015)
63. The Death of Jennifer Kazakos (Dead Souls book 9) (2015)
64. Alice Isn't Well (Death Herself book 1) (2015)
65. Annie's Room (2015)
66. The House on Everley Street (Death Herself book 2) (2015)
67. Meds (The Asylum Trilogy book 2) (2015)
68. Take Me to Church (2015)
69. Ascension (Demon's Grail book 1) (2015)
70. The Priest Hole (Nykolas Freeman book 1) (2015)
71. Eli's Town (2015)
72. The Horror of Raven's Briar Orphanage (Dead Souls book 10) (2015)
73. The Witch of Thaxos (Dead Souls book 11) (2015)
74. The Rise of Ashalla (Dead Souls book 12) (2015)
75. Evolution (Demon's Grail book 2) (2015)
76. The Island (The Island book 1) (2015)
77. The Lighthouse (2015)
78. The Cabin (The Cabin Trilogy book 1) (2015)
79. At the Edge of the Forest (2015)
80. The Devil's Hand (2015)
81. The 13th Demon (Demon's Grail book 3) (2016)
82. After the Cabin (The Cabin Trilogy book 2) (2016)
83. The Border: The Complete Series (2016)
84. The Dead Ones (Death Herself book 3) (2016)
85. A House in London (2016)
86. Persona (The Island book 2) (2016)

AMY CROSS

For more information, visit:

www.amycross.com

AMY CROSS

Printed in Great Britain
by Amazon